Stacey knew herself.

She'd slept with Jake only because she'd hoped for more, and if they ended up with nothing, the wounds would take a long time to heal. Going into the whole thing with her eyes open didn't give her the power she needed to shield her heart.

She felt a ripple of apprehension. She and Jake had slipped so easily into their old familiarity with each other, but seventeen years had gone by. They were different people now. She was a divorced parent, and there were only a handful of life events that could change a person as much as motherhood and a failed marriage. She had to remember how new and untested this all was, and how many pitfalls could lie ahead.

Suddenly she didn't know if seeing Jake was a courageous act on her part...or the most foolish thing she'd ever done.

Dear Reader,

One of the things I love about being an author for Silhouette Special Edition is that we're writing about things that are important in real women's lives. Stacey Handley in *The Couple Most Likely To* doesn't just need to get her relationship with Jake Logan working right, she also needs to balance it with her love for her kids, her dealings with her ex and her ambivalent relationships with her mother and sister. Most women find themselves in this kind of situation at some point in their lives. People need us. We're pulled in six different directions at once. We don't have enough support. Sometimes it's hard.

Stacey's journey in this book represents what I really believe about life and love. If we care enough, we can get it right. Stacey and Jake deserve their happy ending, and I hope you enjoy laughing and crying along with them as they strive to find it.

Lilian Darcy

THE COUPLE
MOST LIKELY TO

LILIAN DARCY

SPECIAL EDITION

Published by Silhouette Books

America's Publisher of Contemporary Romance

Special thanks and acknowledgment are given to Lilian Darcy for her contribution to the LOGAN'S LEGACY REVISITED miniseries

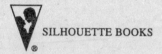 SILHOUETTE BOOKS

ISBN-13: 978-0-373-28049-0
ISBN-10:   0-373-28049-1

THE COUPLE MOST LIKELY TO

LILIAN DARCY

Bestselling romance author Lilian Darcy has written over seventy novels for Silhouette Special Edition, Harlequin Mills & Boon Medical Romance and Silhouette Romance. She currently lives in Canberra, Australia, with her historian husband and their four children. When she is not writing or supporting her children's varied interests, Lilian likes to quilt, garden or cook. She also loves winter sports and travel.

Lilian's career highlights include numerous appearances on the Waldenbooks romance bestseller list, three nominations for the Romance Writers of America's prestigious RITA® Award, and translation into twenty different languages. To find out more about Lilian and her books or to contact her visit www.liliandarcy.com.

Chapter One

The January darkness had already begun to gather outside as Stacey Handley came into the day-care center. The misty drizzle of rain blanketing the region would have reduced visibility on I-5 almost to zero. John was a cautious driver, thank heaven, but the weather conditions on this first Friday of the new year meant he'd probably be late. That and the demands of his job with the Washington State government.

Taking a deep breath, Stacey accepted the inevitable. Even with his usual quick turnaround, her ex-husband would be making the two-hour drive back from Portland to Olympia in full darkness, in slippery conditions, with their precious two-year-old twins strapped in their seats in back.

It wasn't his fault.

It wasn't hers.

It was the fault of their divorce, for sure, and all the mistakes they'd made—including the fact that they'd gotten married in the first place.

In contrast to the gloom outside, the day-care center attached to the Portland General Hospital felt bright and warm. Children's artwork hung on the walls and on colored yarn from the ceiling. Creative imagination buzzed in the home corner, the dress-up area, and the block space.

The place drew Stacey in, giving the usual lift to her spirits. She always loved dropping in here to see Max and Ella during her breaks, and picking them up at the end of the day. In her anticipation at seeing them, she forgot temporarily about the lonely weekend that lay ahead. But for now, she was happy to spend some precious minutes with the twins before John collected them.

Max saw her almost at once and catapulted into her arms. She returned his hug and inhaled the clean smell of his wheat-blond hair, noting that Ella, as usual, was too busy to have noticed her arrival. "Hi, sweetheart," she said to her little boy. "Did you have a good afternoon?"

"Did paintin'."

"Did you? Can I see?" She tried to put him down, but he kept his arms tight around her neck, accidentally pulling on hair that needed a fresh cut.

At this age, he was more clingy than Ella. She always became so absorbed in her play that Mommy often had to join her in an activity for several minutes before she could slowly coax her daughter to let it go. The two were so different in both looks and temperament. Strangers were astonished to discover that they were twins.

Once more, Stacey felt the usual uncomfortable kick of her heart at the thought of letting them go for a whole weekend. Somehow it hadn't seemed so hard last spring after John had first moved to Olympia. Max hadn't yet been walking. They'd both been taking longer naps. When you'd said to them, "Time to get out of the bath," they hadn't thought to protest.

But now, nine months later, they were such a handful. John was a good father and tried his utmost. He usually took them one weekend in three, sometimes one in two, and their divorce had been amicable enough to avoid any dispute over custody or access. Could he really be as watchful as she was, though? Did he fully understand just how fast they could get into trouble?

She glanced toward the window again, and already it looked much darker out there, although it was only just after four. The rain hissed and spat against the glass.

Not rain anymore.

Sleet.

How were those roads?

She needed to get back to work—but she reminded herself that with the twins away she could work late tonight in order to catch up if she was away from her desk for too long now. She could spend a little more time with her children, and coax some hugs from busy Ella, who'd only just seen her and called out, "Hi, Mommy!"

Her heart kicked again.

And then, just when it was the last thing in the world she was thinking about, she heard the voice and saw the face she'd lately been remembering so vividly. Remembering, and trying so hard to prepare for, since she'd dealt with certain employment formalities in the Portland General administrative offices several weeks ago.

Jake Logan.

He stood right there in the day-care center doorway. Gorgeous, ambitious, wide-horizoned Jake. The man she hadn't married seventeen years ago. The man she'd once expected would share the daunting tasks and incomparable rewards of parenthood right along with her. The man who'd left Portland way before she was ready to let him go.

Jake threw her a shocked glance, his recognition instant and obvious. Max had settled himself on her hip as if he planned to stay there all night. Ella trotted toward her for a hug. Stacey would have her arms full by the time Jake reached her.

The relationship between herself and the two small children must be written in every gesture. He would have to realize that they were her kids. In seventeen years she'd been through all sorts of changes, and her emotions had run the gamut. So had his, no doubt. Seventeen years was a long time.

Had he noticed her signature on a couple of the administrative letters he would have received from the hospital? She'd kept her maiden name for work and had gone back to it in her personal life after the divorce. Had Jake realized that coming back to Portland would mean seeing her again?

From his expression, apparently not.

It all seemed too significant.

The burden of being a parent…of caring that much…of risking and losing and hurting…of dealing with two sets of feelings that didn't match…was such a large part of what had separated herself and Jake all those years ago, when they were both still in their teens. She didn't know whether she should still be angry about things he'd said and done. She'd moved on, hadn't she?

Now, trying to keep Max anchored to her hip while she simultaneously scooped Ella up before she began to cry, Stacey muttered under her breath, "It's just the same. I'm carrying the weight. And he's free. Just as he wants to be."

She already knew he wasn't married. Dealing with Portland General Hospital's personnel files had its advantages, sometimes. And when a man like Jake wasn't yet married at the age of thirty-five, it could only be by his own choice.

He looked so good. With Ella's smoochy kiss warm on her cheek, she took in all the ways he'd changed…as well as the ways he hadn't. If he'd been good-looking in her own eyes back then, he would turn any woman's head now. He was thirty-five, the same age as Stacey herself, and while many of his contemporaries had begun to lose their hair and gain at the waist-line, Jake looked fit and strong and confident—a man totally in his prime.

He'd filled out since the age of eighteen, but all of it was muscle, tamed a little—but not much—by the dark tailored trousers and gray-and-white cotton sweater he wore. His dark hair was cut short enough to be neat but long enough to remind her of the way she'd once run her fingers through it. As he passed beneath the beam of a recessed light in the ceiling she saw just the faintest smattering of silver around his temples and behind his well-shaped ears.

He'd entered with Jillian Logan who was a social worker at the adjacent Children's Con-nection and spent a lot of time here in the hospital, as well. Stacey didn't know if the shared last names were just a coincidence. Logan wasn't uncommon, but anyone with that name around this place tended to be related. From the way Jillian had caught her eye, smiled and turned in Stacey's direction, it seemed as if she might soon find out.

"Stacey, hi," she began briskly. She was a very pretty woman with her long brown hair and brown eyes, but usually dressed to give off an impression of professional competence rather than personal warmth. She favored tailored clothing and classic colors, such as today's suit in pale sage green. "I dropped into your office at the wrong moment and discovered my cousin."

Well, that answered the question about their names. The Logan family was very prominent around Portland General Hospital and the adjacent Children's Connection. Jillian's parents had donated an enormous amount of financial and practical support to the fertility clinic and adoption center over the years.

Odd, actually. Stacey had known Jake so well, but she didn't remember any mention of his prominent Logan cousins—not even when she and Jake had been planning their wedding and talking about the guest list.

Jake and Jillian had thrown each other a slightly self-conscious glance, too, as if the word *cousin* didn't feel quite right to either of them.

"He'd like a tour, if there's time, to meet a few people and get his ID card, that kind of thing," Jillian went on, as Stacey lowered both twins out of her arms. "You're starting Monday, Jake?" He nodded and she turned back to Stacey. "Oh, I haven't actually introduced you. Stacey, this is—"

"It's all right," Jake cut in quickly. "Stacey and I already know each other."

He put out his hand to shake hers. Ella had scampered back to the Play-Doh table. Max clung to Stacey's leg, distracting her. She felt the brief squeeze of Jake's hand, warm and dry. The moment bewildered her. Outwardly so ordinary, yet so significant given their history together.

"We've been in touch over his employment contract," she explained quickly to Jillian. Jake had become a successful ob-gyn, specializing in infertility, and Portland General Hospital was fortunate to have him coming to work.

She caught a flash in Jake's green eyes as he took in the way she'd avoided any reference to their high school days, let alone their acknowledged status, back then, as a couple madly in love.

The couple madly in love, in fact.

They'd gotten the official vote from their classmates: The Couple Most Likely To Marry Right Out Of High School, but then life had gotten in the way and it had all fallen apart.

She tensed.

Would he challenge what she'd said? Had Jillian herself been around at that time? Stacey knew she had grown up here. She would have been a couple of years below them in school, however, and Portland was no country town where everyone knew everybody else.

Since Jake had never mentioned his Logan cousins in the past, it seemed likely that the two branches of the Logan family hadn't been close. It seemed equally clear that Jillian had no idea of the tension Stacey could feel between herself and Jake—like the zing of an electric current down a wire.

"Someone said you were over here, Stacey, collecting the twins," Jillian went on easily. "Does that mean you're heading out early today? Because I have a client to see in the I.C.U.—" she looked at her watch "—yikes! Ten minutes ago!"

"It's okay. I'm not heading out early. The twins are going to their father's for the weekend. He's picking them up from here, but I always stop in to say goodbye before they go." Belatedly, she considered Jillian's reference to her client appointment and added, "So go ahead, get up to the I.C.U. I'll finish giving Dr. Logan the tour. After all, it's my job far more than it is yours."

From the corner of her eye, she thought she saw his body tighten. Apparently he'd never noticed her signature on those letters. Not so much of a surprise. They'd only been cover letters for enclosed paperwork. He'd probably tossed them in the wastepaper basket without even looking. In that area, she'd had an advantage. She'd known for weeks that he was coming back into her life.

But she hadn't known how she would feel about it when the time came. Already she realized it was going to be a heck of a lot harder than she'd expected.

"Thanks, Stacey. Jake, I'll see you on the weekend." Jillian touched his arm, but it was a tentative gesture, confirming Stacey's impression that the two of them didn't know each other very well.

As Jillian left, Nancy Allen Logan closed the story she'd been reading to a group of children in the book corner and came over to Stacey, sparing only a faint, uncertain smile for Jake. "*The Cat in the Hat* always goes on longer than I remember. Did you put their overnight bags in Robbie's office, as usual?"

"Yes, with a snack for the ride." She glanced at the clock on the wall. "If John doesn't get here soon, it won't be enough for them and he'll need to stop for a proper meal."

"Uh-oh, junk food alert."

"I know, when you try so hard to give them good food here, and so do I, at home."

Nancy and Robbie Logan ran the day-care center together. He was Jillian Logan's brother, but again the connection wasn't as close as you'd expect. Jillian was one of the Logans' three adopted children, while Robbie had been abducted before Jillian came into the family, when he was just six years old. He hadn't been reunited with his family until just a few years ago. Stacey suppressed a shiver. How did any parent survive something like that? Thinking about it brought out her worst fears.

"Do you need to talk to John before he leaves with them?" Nancy asked.

"No, everything's under control. I'm showing Dr. Logan around the hospital and taking care of some personnel issues he needs in place before Monday. Um…" She hesitated. Did these two know each other? Should she introduce them?

Nancy solved the dilemma with a smile at the man. "You're Jake. Of course. We're meeting you officially on the weekend. I'm looking forward to it."

"It'll be interesting," Jake answered, sounding a little more reserved on the subject. "Jillian made a good case, that it was up to our generation to heal the family rift."

"She must have! Good enough to bring you

to live and work in Portland, and with a close professional involvement with Children's Connection, too."

"We'll see how it works out," Jake said. "I'm a bit of a wanderer, and I'm just renting a place. I can move on in a couple of years if being back here doesn't feel like the right thing. Jillian's the brave one, pushing for this, when it's likely that she'll bear a lot of the consequences if the rift doesn't heal."

"Jillian is always determined to practice what she preaches." Nancy's tone contained the suggestion that sometimes she didn't succeed.

The sound of sudden angry tears from one of the children stopped the cryptic conversation in its tracks. Nancy glanced over to where a junior staff member was trying without success to resolve a conflict between two four-year-olds. She gave a resigned exclamation. "I'd better deal with this one."

Stacey took a breath and turned back to Jake. "ID card first, then the tour?"

"It's your call."

"Let's do it that way. The laminating machine acts up sometimes, and it's already after four on a Friday afternoon. If we have to call the maintenance department to—" She realized she was papering over the tension between them with a level of tedious detail he didn't remotely need, and stopped.

What were Ella and Max doing?

They were absorbed in their play, she saw. She resisted the need to give them another hug and a whole lot of I-love-you-I'll-miss-you messages. She always tried to let them leave without too much fuss when they went for their weekends with John, because it wouldn't be good for them to guess how reluctant she was to have them go. But, oh, it was hard.

What had Jake seen in her face?

"Are you finding this a little harder than you expected?" he asked quietly, opening the day-care center door for her. "Meeting up again, I mean."

"Yes," she admitted honestly. "You haven't changed, and yet…"

"We must be reaching middle age. That's when people start telling each other that they look exactly the way they did in high school, even though it was half a lifetime ago. You do, though, Stacey. You look really good."

"Thanks. So do you."

Her movement past him brought them close. For a moment, she felt his body heat. His male strength seemed to pull on her like a magnet.

Her ex-husband was slighter in build, and Jake himself had been slighter seventeen years ago. This close, she wasn't used to such a powerful contrast between a man's body and her own. It unsettled her way more than she wanted, as did the faint scent of spice and musk that hovered around him.

"It has been a long time," she added. "H-how are you doing?"

"Good. I'm doing great. I'm real good. I'm good."

Jake heard himself repeat his answer to Stacey Handley's simple question not once but a full three times and wondered what the hell his problem was.

Stacey seemed rattled, too, although less rattled than he felt. Her reference to being in touch over his employment contract told him that she must have known he would be starting here, while he'd had no clue that he would be seeing her. Filling in short-term for a colleague in Seattle, he'd landed in an overworked ob-gyn practice. When he'd applied for the position at Portland General he'd thrown most of the necessary paperwork at one of the practice's admin staff, merely scrawling his signature a few times.

Encountering Stacey in the day-care center

felt like an ambush. His heart still beat faster. His head still spun.

By mutual unworded agreement, he and Stacey had lost touch with each other years ago. He wasn't surprised to find she was still in Portland but it was a definite jolt to learn that they'd be working under the same roof. They'd been through too much together to dismiss each other as long-ago high school classmates after a couple of polite questions about kids and careers. They'd defined each other's lives through the choices that had driven them apart, with anger and guilt on both sides.

It was a jolt to see her, all right.

As if he didn't have enough emotional stuff to grapple with, thanks to Jillian Logan's determination to heal the decades-long rift between her family and his. He remembered almost every word of Jillian's approach to him at the medical conference in Seattle several months ago—that stuff about healing and forgiveness, about doing what was right, not what was easy—but was she being naive? Theory could be a lot easier than practice.

Accepting an ob-gyn position at Portland General would be seen by Jillian's parents as an incredibly provocative gesture on Jake's part if he and the other members of the younger generation couldn't convince Uncle Terrence and Aunt Leslie that his intentions were good. Lawrence and Terrence Logan had turned their differing approaches to life into a chasm that had divided the two branches of the family for thirty years. The long-ago kidnapping of Uncle Terrence and Aunt Leslie's eldest son Robbie had only made the chasm wider.

"Let's go to my office and get it all sorted out," Stacey said, and for a horrible moment he thought she was proposing to go over the old ground from their own emotional past, and confront each other with all those things they'd never said to each other at the time.

Then he realized she was still talking about the damned ID card.

They passed through a couple of corridors, a lobby, an elevator. He didn't take any of it in. Had the vague impression of new paint smell and pristine decor which told him the place had very recently been redecorated and remodeled, but realized as Stacey opened her office door that he'd have no idea how to find the departments he needed on Monday.

They were taking a tour in a few minutes, of course, so it didn't matter.

This would mean more awkward time to spend in each other's company, which mattered more.

"Okay, photo first, so if you want to freshen up a little… I mean, you look fine. No spinach between your teeth." Stacey fiddled nervously with the digital camera, and in the enclosed space of her office the awkwardness bounced back and forth between them and seemed to magnify itself.

He had a sudden memory of the time they'd gone to one of those automatic photo booths to get pictures taken for their passports. They'd been planning to spend a year in Europe between high school and college, using a couple of different exchange programs to see places in more depth. They'd both been excited about it.

Imagine. Three months digging up Roman ruins in Italy, as volunteer interns on an archeological site. Six weeks of intensive language lessons in Spain. Picking grapes, staying in cheap hotels, eating where the locals ate, making new friends. They'd gotten the passport pictures, then gone back into the booth to take some more, just for fun. They'd made faces into the camera, standing with heads close together, arms around each other, big, wide smiles.

Oh, lord, it seemed like so long ago!

Was Stacey Handley in any way the same person now?

Was *he?*

When she'd gotten pregnant with Anna she'd abandoned all those plans and dreams as if they'd never existed, and had revealed a hometown-girl side to her personality that had stifled and frightened him.

He'd wanted Stacey.

He wanted to go off into the sunset with her, hand in hand forever.

But the *going off* part was important. He didn't want to settle into marriage and a baby and spend the rest of their dull, suburban lives in Portland. They planned their wedding, but he had to hide how trapped he felt.

And then they'd lost Anna at twenty weeks' gestation. The doctors had called it a miscarriage, although having gone through labor and delivery on the maternity floor right here at this hospital, both he and Stacey had felt it was a stillbirth. No baby could live when it was born at twenty weeks. They didn't know why it had happened. Sometimes, things like this just did.

Distraught, Stacey had wanted to name the tiny baby and he had agreed. It was important. It was necessary.

To this day, he thought of her as Anna. Little Anna. He never helped a patient through the loss of a baby without remembering. Anna Handley Logan. Their lost daughter.

She would have been almost seventeen by now if she'd lived.

But she hadn't.

So Jake had gotten what he wanted. The burden of a settled, responsible future in his hometown had suddenly lifted from his shoulders, but the mix of guilt and grief had been terrible. He'd known he didn't deserve Stacey after this. He'd definitely known he didn't want kids. Not ever. It was too hard. Too frightening. Too horrible. How could she already have begun to talk about "trying again"? He'd started to pick fights with her and push her away and...

Yeah.

Hardly a surprise that their relationship hadn't survived, despite the chemistry and the sense of two souls entwined.

"If you could stand in front of the wall...?" Stacey said.

He stood in front of the wall.

"And smile...?"

He stretched his lips. She took the shot and showed it to him on the little screen.

"Oh, hell!" he muttered. He looked like a rabbit trapped in the headlights of a car. "Could we try that again? I mean, I don't want to scare my patients."

She laughed unsteadily. "I think it was my fault. I'll give you more time."

He shouldn't need more time. It was an ID card photo, for heaven's sake, not the front cover of *People* magazine. "It's fine. I'm ready."

"Um, I'm not. This little green light has to come on. Just a sec." She fiddled again and he watched her while she was unaware.

She looked incredible. Older, of course, but better. Way better. He'd never understood men who couldn't see the beauty in a woman once she passed thirty. Stacey's beauty had a ripeness to it now, an emotional depth behind it that couldn't have been there at eighteen, even though she'd already been mature and grounded back then.

Her figure had grown a little more womanly, with soft curves in all the right places and a grace to her movements that said she knew who she was and was happy with herself. Above her deep blue eyes, her eyelids had tiny, curved creases at their outer corners, as if she had plenty of reasons to laugh and smile. She wore a pleated silk skirt with a pattern like watercolor painting and he could hear the faintest swish of fabric when she moved.

As she examined the uncooperative camera, her honey blond hair fell forward to brush and then mask her face and out of the blue he had another flash of memory, this time about the night they'd conceived Anna, in the backseat of his car after the senior prom. Stacey had had her hair professionally piled on top of her head…it had fallen down as they'd made love…longer back then…tumbling in the dark…glinting with gold…brushing his chest… brushing his—

"Okay, one more time," she said. "Smile!"

He did, and this time when she showed him the photo he thought the whole world would be able to track the erotic direction of his thoughts. "This one shouldn't scare them," he blurted out.

"No." She took a quizzical look at it. "They might want your phone number." She grinned suddenly, making her eyes widen and her arched eyebrows lift higher. Again he remembered. Her smile had always shone at a million watts. The grin didn't last. "Sorry, that was inappropriate." She raked her lower teeth across her top lip.

"It's fine. Forget it." He watched her go to the computer to enter his name and set the machine up for printing and laminating the card. He found the sudden silence unbearable, because it gave him too much time to feel astonished at the fact that all the chemistry was still there. "Back at the day-care center, those were your kids?"

Something to say.

Small talk, in any other situation.

Between the two of them it was anything but.

She nodded, still looking at the screen. "Max and Ella. Uh, the marriage didn't make the grade, though. You probably worked that out."

"Mmm, yes. I was sorry to hear it."

More than sorry, but he couldn't identify the feeling at first.

When he did identify it, he was shocked at himself yet again. At some primal male level, he was basically ready to find out if Stacey needed the man killed—preferably by burying him in the fresh concrete foundations of a large building. Sleeping with the fishes had a certain ring to it, also. How come he'd never thought to cultivate a few useful mob connections for exactly this kind of occasion?

"John has them this weekend," she said. "John Deroy. My ex. He's good. He wants to stay involved. He lives in Olympia, now."

He could see how much she struggled with

this, and it didn't surprise him. She would be the kind of mother who found it difficult to spend any time away from her children, especially since they were so little. He wondered what had gone wrong with the marriage, so soon after what presumably had been a joyful birth.

"So at least when they're with your ex, you get some time to yourself," he said. Too gently. She probably wouldn't be happy to know how easily he'd read her emotions.

She didn't seem to want his empathy or understanding. "Yep, and I par-*tay!*" she said, mocking herself. "Woo-hoo!" She shimmied her hips and did some moves with her hands.

"I have to tell you, your imitation of a party animal is pathetic, Handley."

"Yeah, well, it wouldn't be, Logan, if I was wearing the right shoes." She did a little Charleston dance kick in his direction, as if spiking him with a deadly heel.

They laughed.

And looked at each other.

And stopped, mutually appalled.

Handley and Logan.

Sheesh, had they hit a time warp? How could they have dropped so quickly into the hard-edged teasing routines they'd enjoyed so much back in high school? That was half a lifetime ago. They'd gone in such totally different directions since then. They should have forgotten all of it. The chemistry, the connection, everything.

"Anyhow…here it is," she said, producing the freshly laminated ID card, complete with holographic security logo. She gave it to him, and it still felt warm from the machine. He noted how carefully she avoided touching his fingers during the transaction, as if she didn't dare to risk the burn.

"On to the tour," he said.

They both behaved impeccably.

Mechanically.

Dishonestly.

She showed him the O.R. suite, the maternity floor, the outpatient clinic rooms, the E.R., staff cafeteria and gift shop. "If you need a newspaper, or to mail something." They encountered the head of the ob-gyn department on his way to a C-section delivery, and he and Jake exchanged quick greetings. Stacey spoke to several more people on their journey through the hospital, always with a smile or a question about their day. He could tell that she was both respected and liked. Relied upon, also, judging by the queries she fielded and the cheerfully efficient answers she gave.

"Leave it on my desk… Call me or Hannah next week… Put something in writing—just a few lines—and I can look into it."

Then she took him to the adjacent Children's Connection building, where he would see infertility patients and sometimes supervise the prenatal care of women who planned to give away their babies through the center's highly regarded adoption program.

Highly regarded, but he knew there had been some problems two or three years ago. He'd been working in Australia then, and couldn't remember a lot of detail, nor where his information had come from. Something about babies being kidnapped, IVF mix-ups and adoptions that had emerged as shady. At his job interview, he'd been assured by the Children's Connection's Director of Adoption Services, Marian Novak, that the problems had been sorted out.

If Stacey had more detailed information, she didn't mention it, and he asked her on an impulse, as they crossed back to the hospital, "How long have you been working at Portland General?"

"Since I went back to work after the twins were born. I used to work at Portland University Medical Center, but this position was a step up. It's only part-time for the moment, but I've been told I can upgrade to full-time at some point. For now, it's two days a week, and the occasional evening."

"You probably prefer that anyhow, with the twins."

"It's a good balance," she agreed. "I get to spend quality time with them…but I don't go completely nuts."

The grin came again, practically knocking him off his feet. He liked that she could admit her toddlers sometimes drove her crazy. He found the perfect-mother act that some women put on a little unconvincing.

Again, the more personal direction of their conversation led to awkwardness on both sides and they fell silent.

Jake just didn't get himself into situations like this. He'd traveled so much, had deliberately chosen career steps that gave him variety. He favored relationships that were monogamous and multidimensional and quite passionate while they lasted, but when they were over he moved on.

His previous lovers didn't come back to haunt him.

They moved on, too.

He couldn't remember ever encountering a

former flame in a professional context before this. How did you handle it? How did you resolve the massive disconnect between the practical small talk and the fact that you'd had this person's naked body entwined with yours, and her moans of release hot and breathy in your ear?

Stacey Handley wasn't just any ex-lover, either. She'd always been different.

Because they'd been so young, he told himself quickly.

A moment later, they reached the hospital lobby and she slowed. "You're all fixed up for Monday. You have your parking authorization." She checked off a couple of other details, indicating the printed Portland General Hospital personnel folder she'd given him back in her office. "You're parked in the visitors' lot today?"

"That's right."

"Then you'll want to take that elevator over there." She gestured toward it, helpful and courteous, as if the disconnect wasn't happening for her.

Yeah, but he wasn't fooled.

He obeyed her unstated leave-me-alone-now-please message, said thank-you and goodbye, and headed for the elevator, knowing that there was way more awareness between them than either of them would have expected or wanted, and that she felt it every bit as strongly as he did.

Chapter Two

When Stacey reentered the day-care center, Max and Ella had already left with John.

Dumb of her, really.

She should have returned directly to her office instead of detouring this way in the hope of a final hug, or the chance to see John face-to-face. If she had seen him, she would only have repeated the kind of instructions that always made his hackles rise. Yes, of course he would encourage Ella on the potty, of course he would remember that Max was completely in love with pouring things at the moment, and he'd childproofed his house months ago, so she could give the subject a rest.

"You okay, Stacey?" Nancy Logan approached her. Although the two women didn't see each other away from the hospital, they got on well together. Stacey considered Nancy a friend, and it showed in the other woman's concerned question.

"I'm fine," she answered. "I just hate to think of him driving on the interstate with the kids in this weather after dark."

Nancy patted her arm and gave a wry smile. There was a wealth of understanding in her hazel eyes. "You're like me. You worry too much. It's because of working in hospitals. We never see all the kids who get home safe every night, we only see the ones who don't."

"Stop! Don't even say it!"

"Yes, because I'll scare myself, too." Nancy shivered suddenly. "It's crazy. Is it the dark winter days? I've been worried about Robbie lately, too…" She frowned and glanced over at her handsome husband, who was working in the day-care center office. She didn't explain her reaction. Looked as if she regretted letting anything slip at all.

To change the subject, Stacey said quickly, "Tell me about Dr. Logan. He's your husband's cousin. We—we knew each other in high school but haven't seen each other in almost seventeen years. I didn't like to ask him too many questions about what he's been doing since."

"Mmm, I wish I had more to tell you, but it was only pretty recently that I found out he existed. He's single, he's traveled a lot. You'd know what a successful doctor he is because you've seen his résumé. My in-laws never—but *never!*—speak about that branch of the family, and Robbie and the other kids have learned not to, also. It gets my father-in-law too upset."

"There's obviously some major grievance from the past."

"Which Jillian is determined to heal. She feels like a fraud as a social worker, I think, urging families to work together, when there's such a rift dividing her own. She persuaded Jake to come back to Portland, and I get the impression that wasn't easy. I think we all support her in theory, but it's going to be an emotional business. Speaking of Jillian, here she is again."

Just as had happened an- hour ago, Jillian came briskly in Stacey's direction. This time, she didn't have Jake Logan with her.

"We have a child with behavior problems that she's looking into," Nancy explained quietly. "He's a sweetheart but very hard to manage." She said to Jillian as the social worker reached them, "You're here for Aidan's assessment?"

"Almost not late, this time!"

"I've been telling Stacey about what you're trying to do to bring the Logan cousins back into the family fold. She knew Jake in high school—"

"Stacey, you didn't mention that before," Jillian cut in, her face showing added interest. "Were you good friends?"

"Um…"

Yes, the very best, until we got to the point where we couldn't even be in the same room without anger and hurt overflowing in a huge mess. That's not friendship. Only lovers work that way.

"Sorry, I don't mean to pry," Jillian said, apparently reading too much in her face. "It's just that there's a Logan family potluck dinner happening tomorrow night at his new place, and we both agreed we wanted to dilute the atmosphere by inviting some other people."

"It's a good idea," Nancy agreed.

"Please come!" Jillian urged her.

"Because my last name's not Logan?" Stacey smiled.

"Exactly!"

"Do come," Nancy said. "You don't have the

twins this weekend. And you know Jake. It would be nice for him to see a familiar face since he's newly back in town."

"Give me the details," Stacey said, and she saw from the reactions of both women that they really did want her to come. They were obviously nervous about the event, and she wondered just what had happened long ago to keep the two branches of the family so estranged from one another. "And what do you need me to bring?"

They agreed on a chicken casserole, and Jillian said again that it would be nice for Jake, nice for all of them, because the event should turn into a party, it shouldn't be some dry, sparsely attended family confrontation.

Going back to her office at last, Stacey admitted to herself that her own thoughts about the potluck dinner were far more selfish. She never knew what to do with herself when the twins had gone to John's.

Tonight she would relax with a glass of wine, get a spicy take-out meal that the twins wouldn't have enjoyed, take a hot bath uninterrupted, read a book with soft music playing in the background. Tomorrow she'd run errands without the need for hauling two kids in and out of car seats. She'd do the house cleaning chores she never had time for during the week, then maybe she'd drop in to see a friend.

And by late tomorrow afternoon she'd have gotten all of that need for freedom out of her system and she'd start missing Max and Ella the way astronauts missed gravity, or cave explorers missed light. Her love for them was so powerful and fundamental, it provided the anchor point for her whole universe.

She almost had vertigo when the twins went to John's.

She'd felt an alarming and unexpected degree of vertigo seeing Jake this afternoon, also, but since they were inevitably going to run across each other around the hospital, they both might as well bite the bullet and get used to it now. She would definitely go to the potluck dinner at his place tomorrow night.

"I did as we agreed and invited a few extra people," Jillian told Jake on Saturday evening, at just before six.

She'd arrived at his newly rented house a little early, as she'd promised to do, bearing not only the agreed-upon chocolate mud cakes for dessert, but wine, napkins, extra silverware…most of the party supplies, in fact. She had to send him out to her car to bring in two more bags.

"Great place," she told him, when he returned.

He'd rented a modern log home on a generous acre of land on the hilly outskirts of the city. The property had peace and space and warmth, as well as the easy freeway access to the hospital that he would need when racing to a delivery in the middle of the night.

He'd rented furniture and hired a professional interior designer to add some finishing touches, and in forty-eight hours the place had gone from bare and echoey to fully furnished, before he'd moved his personal belongings in here on Wednesday. Despite the designer's expert eye and attention to detail, Jake wasn't totally happy with the result, however. Something was missing.

"You didn't have to bring all this," he said to Jillian.

"Well, I did have to, with all the extra people." She shrugged and smiled, laughing at herself a little.

"So just how many non-Logans did you invite?"

She ticked them off on her fingers. "Brian and Carrie Summers. They adopted through Children's Connection and it went so well for them that the birth mother, Lisa, is still a big part of their lives. She's become a real friend, so she'll be here, too. And Stacey, whom you know. She and her husband…ex-husband," she corrected quickly, with a regretful expression, "conceived their twins through IVF treatment at the center. That's not a confidence I'm betraying because she's very open about it. And Eric and Jenny asked if they could bring…"

But Jake didn't hear who Eric and Jenny were bringing.

Stacey and John had conceived through IVF.

For some reason, he reacted to this news with a powerful surge of complex emotion. His thoughts whirled. He and Stacey had had no trouble conceiving by accident seventeen years ago. But then Anna's birth had been so horrible. Stacey had bled too much afterward. They'd both been so upset and bewildered. She hadn't realized her postpartum flow was greater than normal, and of course he had no medical knowledge at that point. Neither of them realized soon enough that she had an infection and needed antibiotics.

"Want to help set out the glasses?" Jillian asked, and he nodded absently and set to work, needing only a fraction of his concentration for the mechanical task.

Stacey had had to listen to some typically insensitive opinions from her mother after the birth—that the loss of Anna was "for the best," that in future "maybe you won't be so thoughtless." He'd been rocked by the sense of a burden lifted warring with his genuine grief. They were both a total mess at that point. Had Stacey been scarred physically as well as emotionally by Anna's birth and death? Was this why she hadn't been able to conceive naturally with her husband?

How long had they been trying before they'd resorted to IVF? Treatment for infertility could put an enormous strain on a couple's marriage. The divorce made more sense to him, now.

He looked up from the current task he was working on—arranging platters of crackers, cheese and dips; he didn't even remember Jillian asking him to do it—and there was Stacey herself, following Jillian into the kitchen with a big, glass-lidded casserole dish in her hands. He wanted to confront her with a hundred questions about her marriage, the fertility treatment, the divorce, and almost had to bite his tongue to keep them back.

He'd never felt such a powerful need to make sure that someone was *all right.* It stunned him that he could still feel so protective toward her, that he obviously at some level considered he still had, oh, visiting rights to her heart, the way Dr. Jake Logan, specialist in ob-gyn, had visiting rights to Portland General Hospital.

"Hi, Jake," she said, her eyes huge and bright and…yeah…aware. Nervous. It must show in both of them.

She wore a short-sleeved cream top in some silky, lacy fabric that clung to every curve on her body. A full skirt in a light, patterned fabric swished around her legs and emphasized the swing of her hips when she moved. Her cheeks were pink from the cold outside air between her car and the house, and her honey-toned hair glistened with drops of rain like diamonds scattered over gold.

"Hi." His voice didn't come out right. His body felt angular and awkward, and forbidden parts of it throbbed.

"In the oven?" Jillian asked her, talking about the casserole.

"Yes," Stacey said, "because I made it this morning and it's chilled from the fridge. Don't make the temperature too hot, though."

"Jake?" Jillian gestured at the sleek stainless steel front of the wall oven, with its row of control knobs.

"Do I know how to switch it on? No clue." He stepped toward it just as Stacey put her casserole down on the countertop and did the same.

They stood side by side, studying the situation. He knew he'd swayed too close to her, but he couldn't help it. It felt right, standing close, where he could smell her sweetness and glance down at her pretty profile. He noticed she didn't move away. Her skirt brushed his legs.

Chemistry, again.

Memories.

Needs.

"Hmm," she murmured. "Five separate controls, and none of them have words on."

"This one?" He reached toward it.

"Maybe." She seemed skeptical, and tilted her head. At thirty-five, the fluted line of her neck was still smooth. "But which setting? Do we want plain rectangle, or rectangle with horizontal line near the top, or rectangle with—"

"You're right," he agreed. "What happened to words? And what idiot designs these symbols?"

"I'm going out on a limb, here. I'm going with rectangle with horizontal line near the bottom and Mercedes-Benz symbol in the middle."

"I think the Mercedes-Benz symbol must mean the fan, although I'm sure the car company is appreciative of the publicity."

Stacey laughed, then turned the control to the setting they'd agreed on.

Nothing happened.

She shrugged at him and smiled. Not the million-watt smile, but the crooked one with the dimple in one cheek. Her sarcastic smile. He remembered it very well. Only Stacey Handley produced dimples along with her sarcasm. "Any new theories, Sherlock?" she asked.

Right now, he didn't want theories. He didn't care if it took their combined brainpower another hour to work out how to switch the oven on, as long as it meant they could keep standing close—flirting, remembering the good times instead of the bad—and he could watch her mouth as she spoke.

More people had arrived. What was it about parties that made everyone crowd into the kitchen, when he had that whole professionally decorated great room through the doorway, where they were supposed to congregate? He heard greetings, including the voices of his brothers Ryan and Scott, but didn't turn around.

"This one must be the timer setting," he said to Stacey, as if the oven controls also governed the whole solar system.

"And this is the temperature control. It does actually have numbers, if not words."

They both reached for the remaining knob at

the same time, and Jake's hand landed on top of hers. They turned and looked into each other's eyes. "I—I'm not prepared for this," she said, breathy and gabbling. "I know I'm responsible for it just as much as you are. But I'm not prepared." Still…she left her hand where it was, beneath his. He let the ball of his thumb make slow circles over her knuckles.

"Let's assume it blows up Russia and go with the rectangles instead," he said softly.

"I—I didn't mean the control."

"I know, and you're losing yours a little, aren't you?"

For an answer, she just closed her eyes.

"So am I," he muttered, intending that she should hear, and she did. She pressed her lips together into two tight lines and he wanted to kiss them and soften them and make them part, using his own mouth.

Hell, what was he doing?

He couldn't afford this. Neither of them could. They shared a past but there was no way they could share a future, which meant that following up on his instinctive, powerful, astonishingly familiar attraction just wasn't on. There'd be nowhere for it to go. The attitudes that had separated them hadn't changed. There were feelings they'd never talked about or dealt with.

"Turn it," she said. He couldn't even work out what she meant, for a moment. "I think the first setting has to be for the broiler plate, and the second is for the oven."

"Right. Yes."

"If we put the temperature at about 320…" She did so, and at last the oven responded. They heard a fan start up, and when Stacey picked up the casserole and Jake opened the oven door, they could already feel warmth spilling onto their faces.

"Bingo!" he said.

"Great things happen when two powerful minds work together, Lo—Jake."

She'd almost called him *Logan,* the way she had yesterday in her office, but she'd read the same danger into those old teasing habits as he had, so she'd quickly changed course.

Changing course wasn't enough. She was frowning now, as if playing out memories of the far darker times they'd shared. They needed to get this out in the open—the ongoing attraction, the sense of familiarity, and all the important things they'd never said.

"Let's get a drink and go somewhere where we can talk," he said.

But the timing was impossible. Jillian raised her voice right at that moment. "Everybody?"

The kitchen and adjoining sunroom had filled with people and the noise level of numerous conversations had climbed. If the music he'd put on earlier was still playing, he couldn't hear it anymore, and people hadn't heard Jillian, either.

"Everyone?" she repeated, speaking louder this time. She sounded nervous, as if she didn't want to do this but would do it anyhow, on principle. "Can I have your attention for a minute? Don't worry, it won't take long." The room quieted.

"You're right, Jillian," said her brother Eric. "We should talk about why most of us are here."

"Jake?" She turned to him. "Do you want to recap? Tell everyone what happened when we met up in Seattle?"

"I think you should do that," he told her. "You were the one who approached me, and I know that took some guts, under the circumstances."

He heard a tiny sound from Stacey, still standing beside him. She didn't move, but she looked interested and curious—as well she might. He felt awkward about the fact that everyone—his brothers, his cousins, their partners, spouses, dates and friends—would see the two of them standing like a couple at such a significant moment.

Jillian nodded. "All right," she agreed quietly, then raised her voice again. "Many of you know this part. I saw Jake's name on a conference program in Seattle a few months ago, and realized from his looks and his age and his biography in the conference program that he had to be one of *those* Logans. You know the ones, Robbie, Eric, Bridget? The ones we never speak about? The ones we never see? The ones who might as well not exist?"

They nodded. The family knew. Some people didn't.

"I listened to Jake give his presentation on infertility and emotional well-being, and at first I thought I'd just sneak out afterward and not say anything—the way we've not said anything to or about Lawrence Logan and his family almost our whole lives. But then I thought, 'What's wrong with this picture?' Here I was, a social worker, listening to a doctor talk about family dysfunction and family healing. And the doctor was my own cousin. And I hadn't met or spoken to him *ever,* because my father couldn't forgive his father for things that had happened twenty and thirty years ago."

"Thirty *years?*" murmured his brother

Scott's date, as if dinosaurs had still roamed the earth.

"So when the session was over, I went up to him," Jillian continued. "My legs were shaking. I had no idea what kind of a reception I'd get."

"But you came up to me anyhow, Jillian." Jake picked up the story. "For those of you who don't know this—"

He threw a brief glance at Stacey, but there would be others, he knew. His brother Ryan's girlfriend, Brian and Carrie Summers, their friend Lisa. There were several more unfamiliar faces, also. His stepsister Suzie was here and had brought a date, as had Scott. His cousin Eric's wife, Jenny, had brought her brother Jordan, a high-power corporate attorney.

"Thirty-one years ago, our cousin Robbie was kidnapped." He saw Nancy squeeze her husband's hand and frown at his words. "It was a devastating event for my uncle and aunt, as you can imagine. My parents wanted to help, but Uncle Terrence couldn't accept that kind of support from them. As brothers, their life choices and priorities had always been at odds, and I know my uncle was racked with a belief that if he'd been a better father, Robbie would never have disappeared."

There was a murmur from the listeners.

"My father was hurt by the repeated rebuffs," Jake continued, "and when he went on, a decade later, to write his two bestselling books on family values he was careless in the case studies he chose. One of them was strongly based on his brother, Terrence, and if there had been any chance of reconciliation before the books were published, there certainly wasn't once they achieved their stellar success. *Hardest to Forgive* stayed at the top of the *New York Times* Nonfiction Bestseller List for forty-three weeks."

Beside him, Stacey made another sound. She'd read it. Millions of people had. It had surpassed even the sales of his dad's first book, *The Most Important Thing.*

"There were some crucial sections in the second book which Dad intended as an attempt to reach out to his brother, but unfortunately the timing was bad."

"With both books the timing was bad," Jillian said. "A false lead had come up regarding Robbie's whereabouts. I know my parents received several fresh blows over the years. Although we all shared their anguish, we were just kids. I can't even imagine what it must have been like."

At the back of the room, Robbie nodded,

while his wife, Nancy, squeezed his arm. Jake had only been four years old at the time, but the suffering on both sides of the Logan family had been fierce for years afterward. He still had some distant memories of phone calls and police cars and angry confrontations—of his parents trying to help his aunt and uncle, his mother bringing casseroles, his father wanting to hand out fliers, and all their efforts being rebuffed.

"In his anguish over Robbie," he continued, "Uncle Terrence took everything Dad had written in the opposite way to what he'd intended—as a further indictment of my uncle's choices, his marriage, and the way he was raising his kids. I can understand my father's message. The thousands of letters he's received over the years from around the world attest to its value. I'm proud of him and what he achieved, but my uncle and his family did suffer because of that book."

"We all did," Eric Logan said. "Word got around. I've seen copies of both books with the fictional names Uncle Lawrence gave us foot-noted by hand with our real names. Our friends' parents passed the book around the way people used to with dirty magazines in high school."

Bridget picked up the story, while Jillian stayed significantly silent, Jake noted. He had the impression she'd reached her personal comfort threshold and was ready to leave the emotional revelations to others. "Kids would ask us if he beat us," Bridget said, "and what was wrong with our mom, and why didn't they just get a divorce, and was my dad the worst father in the world, if it said so in a book that millions of people had read."

Eric put his arm around his sister. "People willfully took the book's message in the wrong way, when it referred to our family. A lot of people were very happy for us to prove single-handed that money can't buy happiness. I heard whisperings that Robbie hadn't been kidnapped at all, that he was buried in our basement and our parents had put him there."

Nancy clicked her tongue in distress and she and Robbie held each other more tightly.

"I was the youngest, which spared me the worst treatment," Bridget said, "but as I grew older I could understand why Dad was angry."

"And yet we've all lost out, over the years," Jillian came in. Her tone edged toward clinical. "I think people always do, when there's that level of family conflict. I want to heal the rift—in this generation, and hope-fully even between our parents. Over coffee at the conference, I convinced Jake to come back to Portland. This potluck supper is our first attempt at reconciliation."

"I'm glad it's happening," said Scott. "I'm glad to be a part of it. Jillian and Jake, thanks." He put his hands together and began to applaud, and soon everyone had joined in.

"Your parents aren't here," Stacey said beside Jake, when the applause died. The story had drawn her in. He could see the troubled emotion in her face. Because she'd never felt close to her own parents or her sister? Jake wondered. He knew they'd moved to San Diego some years ago.

Jillian pulled a wry face in answer to Stacey's question. "No. Well. First things first. We'll have to work up to it."

"Were they asked?"

"My father and stepmother are in New York for a few days," Jake said, "Visiting my brother L. J."

"And our parents didn't want to know," Jillian put in. "Especially Dad."

"I think it's his problem, Jillian. Time heals, but he won't let it do so in this case." Bridget hugged her older sister. "I agree with Scott. I'm so glad you've done this."

The formality began to fragment and the noise level rose again. Stacey remained at

Jake's side. "I had no idea about the rift in your family," she said, when no one else was close enough to hear. "You never told me."

"It didn't seem important to me back then."

"But it does now? It must, or you wouldn't have come back to Portland." She stayed silent for a moment as she thought, then her face changed suddenly. "No. That's right. Yesterday you told Nancy if family tensions run too high, it's very easy for you to leave. Portland might be your hometown, but it's a way station for you, just like any other place, just as you always wanted."

He couldn't mistake the anger in her voice, or the shift in her attitude. She didn't think highly of the way he ran his life, and she took it personally.

"Stacey—"

Stacey gave a mechanical smile and didn't let herself meet Jake's eye. "Excuse me, Jake, I'm going to grab some food now and say hi to Nancy."

"Hey, look, don't you think we need to—?"

No. She didn't think they needed to do anything.

She knew *she* needed to find some space. She was furious with herself.

And, yes, as Jake had picked up, she was angry with him, too. He hadn't changed…and she should have understood this at once. She should never have *flirted* with him over the oven controls, letting the old attraction show so openly.

She found it disturbing enough that the attraction still existed. To act on it in any way would be asking for trouble. He stood close, a little threatening in the way he confronted her. What did he want? Honesty? To dig up the past?

"Let me breathe, Jake. It's a mistake, thinking we have anything left for each other after all this time. Anything except anger and regret."

He gave a tight nod. "You're probably right. I just wanted to talk."

"Well, I don't." She turned away from him and looked for Nancy across the room.

She'd been captured by all the wrong memories, yesterday and this evening. The good memories. Memories of how she and Jake had once connected to each other with humor, and through the sizzle of teasing laced with awareness. Nothing's funnier than a joke between two people who want each other, no matter how lame the actual lines. She and Jake used to laugh all the time, while their blood sang with wanting.

So help her, her blood still sang with wanting, but she had to *forget* about that and focus on all the ways he'd hurt her, and all the signals that he hadn't changed. She spent the next hour talking to other people, helping to serve the hot food.

Anything to avoid getting too close to Jake.

Chapter Three

The situation was ironic, Jake decided.

He'd come back to Portland to heal one rift, only to face another one. And to be honest, in his adult life he'd been affected a heck of a lot more by what had happened between himself and Stacey than by the fact that his father and his uncle didn't speak to each other.

Am I going to let this happen?

Am I going to let us go the whole evening without talking about what we went through together, and how we feel now? I want to say Anna's name out loud, to the one person who'll understand how sweet and sad it sounds.

No. He wasn't going to let it slide.

He couldn't.

They had to talk.

He looked across the room at Stacey. He'd been tracking her the whole evening, for a good two hours at least, although he'd tried not to let anyone see it—especially Stacey herself.

To his eyes, she was the star of the whole gathering. The prettiest. The warmest. The best listener. The one who set up the most unlikely conversational pairings—such as the one between his brother Ryan's supercilious, bored-looking girlfriend and his cousin Eric's quiet wife, Jenny.

"Anitra, Ryan tells me you're studying for a law degree, part-time, while you model," Jake had heard her say, while pretending he wasn't listening. "Jenny, you're an attorney and I know you were juggling a lot of commitments at one stage. Any tips for Anitra?"

Now Anitra was laughing with Jenny, in the middle of one of those very female conversations where they're both nodding like crazy and going, "Oh, I know! Oh, absolutely! Oh, I totally understand!" the whole time.

Jillian and her friend Lisa Sanders were talking together very earnestly. Stacey had been a part of their conversation for some minutes, also. Lisa seemed a little upset and agitated. Stacey had listened intently to what she'd said, nodding and frowning. Now Jake heard Jillian say in a decisive way, "You cannot have something like this hanging over you, Lisa, and neither can Carrie and Brian. Get the legal situation checked out. If there's any chance that your ex could invalidate the adoption…"

Lisa chewed on her lip. "My ex. I can't believe we were ever involved. It seems a lifetime ago. And I can't believe he would try to mess with all our lives like this, just because he thinks there's something in it for him." She shook her head, sounding distressed, and Jake realized he should move farther away from what was obviously a very personal conversation.

Meanwhile, Stacey had retreated to his kitchen to load the dishwasher, which unfortunately matched the oven and had similar cryptic controls.

His cue, he decided, heading in that direction. "Try the Mercedes-Benz symbol, Stace."

"Yeah, I would," she answered, straightening. If her cheeks had been a faint, pretty pink before, they were flushed now. It suited her, hinted at her emotional nature. "Only there isn't one."

"Leave the dishwasher," he growled at her. "I want to talk to you."

"The feeling isn't mutual, Jake, right now." She hunched her shoulders, and hugged her arms across her front. "We—we flirted before, and we shouldn't have. It was irresponsible and meaningless and just dumb. If you think I'm backing off fast…you're right! I don't want to talk."

"Don't you think this is the best time?" He stepped closer, because he didn't want people to hear this. "When seeing each other again has brought our emotions so close to the surface?"

"Why do we have to talk at all? We haven't, for seventeen years, and we've done okay."

"Have we? Have we really done okay? I think it's all still there, underneath. I think it's still affecting us."

"Well, of course." Her voice dropped low. "There's still barely a day goes by that I don't think about Anna…."

There it was. The sad sound of her name that he'd needed to hear, and that reproached him every single time. In his mind, he could see her, the tiny, tiny form, the black silky hair, the paper-thin translucent skin, those brief, fluttering movements she'd made before—

Stop.

Just stop.

"...especially since I had the twins," Stacey was saying.

"Not just Anna," he forced himself to argue. "The choices we made afterward. The things we turned our backs on."

"*You* turned your back on."

"You, just as much."

"I don't see it that way." She sounded very stubborn, with a good bit of bravado in the mix.

"No?" he challenged her. "We always talked about seeing the world, and yet you're still here in Portland with a failed marriage, stuck in a dreary suburban rut...."

She flinched, and he wished he'd chosen his words better.

Then she lifted her chin and returned the attack, which shouldn't have surprised him. "So making a family means being in a rut, does it, Jake? What about you? Some people wouldn't call what you've done with your life widening your horizons, they'd call it running away."

"They'd be wrong. I like my life very much."

"Good for you." She blinked back sudden tears. "And I like mine. There. We've talked. We've told each other we're happy. We've defended our choices. That's enough, isn't it?"

"Stacey…"

"It's enough," she repeated. "Thank you for this." She waved vaguely at the gathering, which was still going strong after two or three hours. "I like your family. I've had a good time. I'm glad Jillian invited me. But I'm going home."

He didn't try to argue, but only because he'd already decided to tackle their talk a different way.

The worst part about Stacey's rare evenings out when the twins were away was that she had to come back to an empty house. She'd left the heating turned up and a couple of lights on in strategic places, so the space was cozy enough. Her garage opened directly into a mudroom off the kitchen, which meant there was no interval of cold and vulnerability as she walked between the car and the house, but still it felt lonely and wrong.

So much in her life was right. Her children, her job, her house, her friends.

This part of it wasn't.

She'd never planned for a life in which she had to come home at night alone. She liked the warmth of people around her, and found it nourishing. As a poor substitute for actual human contact, she checked the answer machine and found a message from her sister, Giselle, which was unusual. Stacey was the elder by five years and they'd never been all that close. Giselle had only been thirteen when she and Mom and Dad had moved to San Diego.

On the machine, she sounded perky and busy. "Hi-i, Stacey! Just calling. No reason. Talk to you soon. Bye-ee!"

No other messages.

Which was good, because it meant that everything must be running smoothly for John with the twins.

Stacey looked at the clock on the microwave—9:42. "What?" she complained to the green numbers. "You leave me with an hour between now and bed, and no suggestions about what I should do? You couldn't have made it 10:25?"

No reply from the clock.

She made herself some hot chocolate, lit the gas fire—more for the companionship of its cheerful blue and orange flames than for its warmth—and put on a DVD.

About twenty minutes later, she'd gotten comfortable when her doorbell rang, which spooked her a little at this time of night—until she looked through the peephole.

She should have known.

Jake.

Heart sinking, she opened the door for him, with a brief, "Hi," then stood back in silence for him to walk past her into the house. Clearly, he'd meant what he said about needing to talk. Even outside of rush hour, his place was a solid twenty-minute drive from here. He must have left his guests with Jillian to act as hostess. What kind of excuse had he made?

He didn't intend to waste any time getting to the point, it seemed. She offered several beverage options, hot and cold, but he waved them all away. She ushered him toward the fire, but he ignored her and paced up and down the patterned Persian rug instead.

"I'm sorry," he said. "I shouldn't have said what I did about you being in a rut. It wasn't exactly the best start I could have made."

"Start to what?"

"We have to say this stuff, Stacey! We're going to keep seeing each other around the hospital. Nancy and Jillian both think of you as a friend, and I'm working on thinking of them as family. The connections are there, and ongoing. We ended in such a mess seventeen years ago. We're a lot older now. You know I loved you—"

"Did you? You loved me? You'd claim that?"

"Do you doubt it?"

"You pushed me away! You picked fights. I was the one who finally said *It's over,* yes, but you *made* me say it, Jake. You didn't rest until you'd goaded me into it!"

He stopped pacing in the middle of the rug, pinned by her words. They'd hit home. She could see it.

"You manipulated me into saying it," she went on, "as the punch line to a massive fight, and you left me with the guilt when I did. We conceived Anna together, and we lost her, and then you manipulated the relationship so that *I* was the one who couldn't let the loss bring us closer. It took me a long time to see all of that, but I know it's the way it was. The only thing I don't understand is why. If you're telling me you did love me…"

"Of course I did."

"But you stopped loving me after Anna died? Because you wanted to be free?"

"After Anna died, I was never going to be free," he muttered, so low that she wasn't convinced she'd heard him right.

"Well, it's the only reason I can come up with." She turned toward the gas fire, needing to look at those leaping flames, instead of Jake's frowning face.

"Is it?" he said.

"The evidence is there in the life you've lived since, Jake." She didn't turn to face him again, but felt him move closer. "I've seen your résumé. No wife. No kids. You don't stay in one place for longer than two or three years. You've worked all over the world. Clearly that need for newness and change and movement runs deep. And it angers me that you couldn't be honest about it. You wanted your freedom, but you couldn't say so. You had to turn me into the bad guy, instead." She shook her head. "I had the same thing from my mother my whole life, growing up. I was the disappointing daughter, the one who messed up, while Giselle was perfect. I can fall into the role of bad guy *sooo* easily, Jake. Very convenient for you. And yet—you didn't put me there on purpose? If you did—" she shook her head again "—then we really have nothing to say."

"You weren't this angry yesterday, or earlier tonight."

She laughed. "No, because believe it or not, in a rut or not, I do have a life—one that I find very satisfying, by and large."

"Tell me."

"My job, my kids, my friends, my house, my hobbies. I haven't spent the past seventeen years dwelling on grievances. I'm a pretty positive person. At first, when I saw you and talked with you, I remembered the good times. The connections."

Oh, boy, did she remember the connections! He'd moved to stand beside her now, and they both watched the fire. Every cell in her body seemed to pull toward him. What was it about this one man? She had to take a breath to steady herself before she could continue.

"Now, though, when you tell me that I'm in a rut, and say that you did love me… Yes, I'm angry. It's confusing and upsetting. And I really don't understand."

She had to wait a long time for his reply. The fire purred faintly, and the room was so quiet that she could hear the whir of the DVD player, which she'd left on the pause setting. Finally, he spoke. If that DVD player had been any louder, she wouldn't have heard.

"I pushed you away because I felt so damn guilty, Stacey."

Jake heard the words that came out of his mouth after the long silence and didn't know if he could follow through with the full truth, even now. Was this what he'd meant by talking? Had he intended to make this much of a confession?

He'd driven here without rehearsing his lines, without much rational thought at all. He'd just known he needed to see her again tonight, not wait for some awkward moment when they ran into each other at the hospital.

As soon as he'd entered her house he'd felt the old attraction flare once again. He'd barely taken in the decor, just a vague impression of warmth and color and quirkiness, the kind of detail you promised yourself you'd take a closer look at next time.

And then the first thing he'd done was apologize, because there was so much he regretted when it came to Stacey and their shared past. But could he talk about it?

"Guilty?" she echoed. "Because Anna came too soon? How was that your fault? The doctors told us—"

"Because it let me off the hook. It opened the door to the original plan, the one we'd had to let go of when we found out you were pregnant. You know the saying. Be careful what you wish for."

Tears filled her eyes. "You *wished* for—"

He swore harshly. "No! Of course I didn't wish for us to lose Anna! But I would never have chosen at that age to get married and be a father and settle down in Portland, Stacey. I wanted you, but I didn't want the whole traditional package. Not then. Not at eighteen."

"And now?"

"We're not talking about now. But, no, I don't see myself ever going that route, I have to say."

"Because it's boring? Narrow?"

"Because it's…"

Too scary, and too hard.

Anna had taught him this. Most men— boys—have pretty simplistic attitudes to life at eighteen. Love is love. Grief is grief. Freedom is freedom. You want what you want. No ambivalence. No excuses. Until Stacey's pregnancy he'd never imagined you could tear yourself in two with such conflicting, opposing emotions—emotions that simply had no way to coexist. Loving Stacey became a burden. Loving Anna was a burden, also, and every bit as heavy.

"Because it's just not for me," he finished after a moment. "It's still not. And it definitely wasn't for me back then. There were times— a lot of times—when I just wanted the whole situation to go away. Like for some superhero to fly up into space—" he mocked himself with words and tone "—and reverse the rotation of the earth so that time would spin itself back to the moment before I *didn't* pick up a pack of condoms the night of the prom, or something. It wasn't logical. It was never logical or rational or thought out, Stacey. I just wanted the situation to go away," he repeated.

"And then it did."

"And then it did."

"And I was racked with grief, while you—"

"I was, too. Never doubt that! Only I didn't have the right to be, I only had the right to feel guilty, because at some level I'd made it happen. Again, not rational. We were both in a mess. For a while, I tried to pick up the idea of us traveling, going to college together somewhere different. Like New York."

"I remember you talked about New York."

"You weren't interested. You didn't want to know. You wanted me to stay at Portland State."

"I needed *time,* for heaven's sake!"

"I know," he answered quietly. "I just couldn't see it then. Of course you did. But even if I'd given it to you, I'm not sure that it would have helped, because I wasn't ever going to let myself be happy with you after we lost Anna."

"Because you didn't think you deserved to get what you'd always wanted—the two of us *and* the wide horizons."

"That's right."

"Oh, Jake…" She didn't sound angry anymore.

"I picked the fights. I did push you away. I'm so sorry about that, Stacey, believe me. When you told me we were finished, it hurt like hell, but I felt like it had to happen. It was inevitable. There was a relief, too. Cosmic justice had been served."

"Jake…"

"I was eighteen. *We* were eighteen." To both of them, it sounded so impossibly young.

He put his arm around her and she leaned in, not away. Her head dropped to his shoulder. They stared at the flames. He felt a cloak of peace settle over his shoulders. Peace and trust.

"Tonight, when I said her name…" Jake revealed. "You're the only one I can say her name to, Stacey. My mom and dad, maybe, but it's still not the same."

"No. It wouldn't be."

Her bare arm felt warm beneath his hand. Her hip bumped his and he realized their thighs were pressing together, separated only by the fabric of his jeans and her frothy skirt. None of this was about sex, though, it was about shared pain and mutual support.

"I said something about her to my mother, once," she said quietly, after a minute. "Maybe five years ago? I used her name. *After Anna died.* Do you know what Mom said?"

"Tell me."

"'*Who's Anna?*' Mom had forgotten that we ever named her."

"She'd forgotten? The name of her own lost granddaughter?"

"I know. It felt like a punch in the gut."

He turned her into his arms and said against the softness of her hair, "You are a miracle, Stacey."

"Because I'm not like my mother?" she whispered.

"Yes!"

He couldn't speak.

He had more to remember.

Those awful moments when they'd had to break the news to their respective parents that Stacey was pregnant. They'd announced their plan to marry at the same time. He knew his parents had had doubts and concerns, but they'd expressed them in the context of their love and support, and they'd swallowed a lot of their fears, ready to just be there, rather than preach.

Stacey's mother had been far more vocal, all of it a variation on the theme of, "How could you do this to me?" How could Stacey and Jake embarrass Trisha Handley with a teen pregnancy in front of her friends? How could they make her a grandmother, when she was only forty-three? And if they thought they'd be able to dump the baby on her for free child care whenever they felt like it, it wasn't going to happen, because Bob Handley's company was transferring him to San Diego in the spring, thanks very much, so she wouldn't be around.

He wasn't surprised that Stacey had chosen to stay in Portland when her parents and her younger sister had moved. She'd toughed out her freshman year at Portland State, earning a couple of incompletes when they lost the baby, and she'd stayed on there after Jake himself had left town. She'd moved into one of the college dorms when her parents sold their house, continued her degree part-time while she worked, and, he suspected, had remained independent of her family ever since.

He might question her choices and her priorities, but he would never question her courage.

He held her closer, feeling the heat from the gas fire against his legs. She made no move to push him away, and time seemed to slow while the universe shrank to this one point of sanity and rightness. He and Stacey, holding each other, seventeen years too late. He pressed his cheek against hers, needing the touch of her skin. She rubbed her face against his jaw like a cat, and he could smell the soft, flowery fragrance she must have dabbed below her ears at the beginning of the evening.

"Oh, Jake..."

He didn't intend to kiss her. He really didn't. But she pressed her lips to his cheek...it wasn't an intentionally sexual or inviting gesture, and yet it had the same effect. This close, he wanted her, and his body reacted to the signals she sent, even if she didn't know she was sending them.

"Stace..." He turned his head the necessary inch and found her mouth, sweet and soft, while it was still imprinting those chaste, emotional kisses on his skin—the kind of kisses she might have given a crying child. "Stace..."

The kiss changed.

She made a small sound of protest in her throat.

Protest or need, he couldn't tell.

Mixed signals.

He interpreted them the way he wanted, supported by the evidence of her arms holding him tighter, her body going pliant and soft, her lips parting to welcome him in. Their tongues met and swirled together, and he remembered. They used to kiss for hours, long ago. They burned each other up.

Tonight, she tasted of chocolate and wine and her hair smelled like strawberries. He felt the push of her breasts and the bump of her hips. He slid his hands over the back of her skirt, loving the taut curves he could feel beneath the swishy fabric.

Her fingers stroked his neck, ran up into his hair. His mouth wasn't enough for her and she kissed his whole face—his closed lids, his cheekbones, his forehead and back to his eager lips—as if she had to learn every contour by heart while she could.

They both grew breathless, and the heat of the fire became totally swamped by the throbbing heat in his groin. He wanted to pull off her clothing, see her body, feel the weight of her breasts in his hands, suckle her until she gasped and cried out, take her right here, thrusting into her swollen sweetness without another word or a pause for thought.

If they were going to stop…

They *had* to stop.

She thought so, anyhow.

She pulled away with a gasping breath and held his face between her hands, studying the expression in his eyes.

Which was probably pretty easy to read.

"You have a bad effect on me," she said.

"Yeah…?"

Sounded like a nice idea. How much bad effect did she want? He had plenty, he could give her a ton of it. And her mouth was so close.

"Your body switches off my brain."

"Brains need a break, sometimes."

"Not tonight, Jake. Not with you."

"Not even when it's obvious how much we both want it? Not even when we think about how good it once was?"

"Especially not then." In her eyes, clouds crossed over the blue. "I—I don't even know why we're standing here like this. Why I let you kiss me. Or why I kissed you back." She muttered something under her breath. Swearing at herself?

"Stacey…"

"Should I still be angry with you? I have no idea. You talked about how you felt back then. Is that enough? Do you hear how I sound? I'm at sea when it comes to you. I don't know what I do feel or what I should feel or what I want to feel."

"No…"

"It stopped being simple after Anna died and I don't think it'll ever be simple again. If seventeen years of complicated living didn't solve it, I'm not sure what could." She took a couple of shuddery breaths and then he felt her shoulders lift and square. "Jake, let's please not get ourselves into a situation where this can be repeated." She dropped her hands from his face.

"I'm sorry," he said again. "I'm sorry. It's what we missed before, isn't it? What *I* missed. The saying sorry. It's seventeen years too late, but for what it's worth, after what we've said to each other tonight, I'm so sorry."

"For what?"

"For turning you into the bad guy when we split up. You're right. I mean, I don't think that was my motivation—to let myself off the hook—but I can see that the end result was the same. You felt as if it was your fault, and it wasn't. It's funny how two people can see the same situation from such opposite angles."

He still held her loosely, but wasn't surprised a few seconds later when she peeled herself out of his arms and put some distance between them. "I guess we did need this. The talk. But you should probably get back to your family dinner."

"Kicking me out?"

"Not exactly. But I do think you should go." Her blue eyes still glittered with emotion.

"What are we left with then, Stacey?"

She spread her hands. "You tell me. We're

going to see each other pretty much every week, for as long as you stay in Portland. There should be an agreement. Daggers drawn? Nasty e-mails? Frosty formality?" Her humor attempted to undercut the lingering atmosphere, but didn't fully succeed.

"Listen, I want us to be…if not friends, then amicable colleagues. We can manage that, can't we?"

"Sure." She gave a bright nod. "I can do amicable. I've had practice."

"Yeah?"

"My parents. My sister. My ex. I'm the queen of amicable. I wrote the manual. I can do amicable in my sleep, with both hands tied behind my back."

"You're telling me that's not what you want?"

"Not at all. I just wonder sometimes if that's the best I can hope for." She looked him in the eye. "Sometimes *amicable* is just code for *superficial,* don't you think?"

Chapter Four

"And now I'd like to introduce Dr. Jake Logan, who's going to talk to you about the different treatments we offer," Stacey said, "as well as outlining some of the steps you might go through during the process of assessing which treatment will be the most appropriate. Dr. Logan has come to us following previous stints in Seattle and Denver, as well as a fellowship in Melbourne, Australia, where one of the world's first successful in vitro fertilizations took place."

She gestured to him and smiled, while he nodded and rose to his feet.

"We're very happy to have him working with us here at Portland General Hospital and the Children's Connection," she continued, "And if you choose to come to us for your fertility treatment, we're sure you'll be happy, too."

She stepped back from the podium as the audience of around twelve couples applauded. Jake stepped forward, with everyone's eyes upon him. Stacey held her breath. She hadn't heard him speak in public since the speech he'd made as high school valedictorian, and not all medical professionals could express themselves clearly to lay people.

The hospital ran regular information evenings on infertility, and she was responsible for coordinating speakers, collating handouts and generally making sure the evenings ran smoothly. It was important that the sessions were a success because couples in the Portland region had choices about where they could go for treatment.

She and John had come here for theirs, while things were still settling down following the scandals of a few years ago, and she knew how close the place had come to being destroyed. Now, both the hospital and the associated Children's Connection wanted to maintain and build their high profile and their solid reputation in the area of fertility treatment, and it was part of her job to make sure this happened.

"One of my maternity patients in Australia used to tell me that all she had to do to get pregnant was use her husband's toothbrush," Jake began. He paused for the ripple of laughter, and Stacey began to relax. This medical professional could hold an audience. She should have known.

"It won't surprise you that I helped her give birth to her sixth child," he continued. "For all of you, however, it's begun to seem as if a tooth-brush isn't going to cut it in the conception de-partment. It's a disappointment that is often intensely personal and difficult to face, and we're going to have to work with you to achieve what you want. You already know it might not be an easy journey."

He looked good up there, Stacey thought, as he continued to speak.

He wore dark trousers and a pale gray business shirt with his hospital ID card pinned to the pocket—the brand-new ID card in which the photo she'd taken last Friday seemed to capture his innate aura of warm, masculine sen-suality. His hair caught the light when he moved and she glimpsed the silver threads she'd noticed last week.

When he smiled, the audience felt his warmth, and when he told them that this hospital's infertility program would give them the right support as well as results on par with any program in the country, they believed him.

How could a man who spent his whole pro-fessional life promoting parenthood be so certain that he didn't want this role for himself?

Stacey felt the sting of sudden tears.

Was it the loss of Anna? It must be. The sadness of it caught at her heart.

What a terrible responsibility to lay on their innocent child!

"You didn't do that for me, sweetheart," she whispered to their daughter inside her head. "You showed me the opposite—that love is worth any amount of loss, that there can be a whole world of meaning in one tiny heart. And I'm so grateful to you for it."

Her heart ached for Jake, suddenly, and any lingering anger disappeared. How could she be angry with him, when he'd lost so much more than she had? Was there any way she could communicate to him all the positive things that Anna had given her?

Thinking about it, she only knew that she had to try. The need burned in her like a flame.

Somehow, she owed it to Anna's memory, and to all the good qualities in the man himself.

Forget "amicable." She was so tired of amicable. Her ex-husband, her parents, her sister… She couldn't add Jake's name to the list. She had to try for more.

Jake pressed the control he held in his hand so that the computerized slide presentation unfolded smoothly to illustrate each point he made, and he paused several times for questions because he knew it was best to deal with them in the right context. Couples nodded and murmured at each other. People who'd been frowning when the session began were smiling now. He was so good at this!

Then she saw him frown toward the side of the room. She glanced over to the supper table and realized that the big electric urn had begun to boil too rapidly, creating a distracting sound for Jake and for those seated nearby.

She jumped up and turned it lower, checking that tea bags and sachets of coffee, milk and sugar, crackers and cookies were all set out in the right way. Jake nodded in her direction, and the brief eye contact was enough to throw her thoughts back to Saturday night all over again.

Only three days ago.

She'd slept badly that night, nagged by contradictory emotions and wrapped in vivid memories of their kiss. The next day she hadn't known what to do with herself and had frittered the time away until it was time to leave for Olympia to pick up the twins. She'd told John four o'clock, but as usual she reached his house early, her heart lifting in anticipation.

She always had the impression that John felt a little relieved, as he saw her pull into his driveway, to know that Max and Ella would soon be off his hands. He wasn't having them again until the last weekend in January—almost three weeks away—and this time they'd agreed that she would drive them north late on Friday afternoon, and he would bring them home.

"They were great," he'd told her. "We went to one of those play-zone places yesterday. Tired them out nicely for their naps, while I managed to grab a coffee and skim the newspaper. I wish Max would eat better, though. Plain macaroni, apple and peanut butter, that was about it for the whole two days. We had a standoff at dinner last night over the fish fingers and peas."

"Who won?"

"Nobody. He didn't eat the peas, he cried and drummed his heels on the floor for twenty minutes, and he didn't get dessert."

Stacey resisted the temptation to believe she could have resolved the conflict more successfully, because in all likelihood she wouldn't have. Max was stubborn about food. Ella was stubborn about everything else.

John tried hard.

He'd tried hard when the two of them were first going out together. He'd swept her off her feet— swept away her doubts—with the most romantic springtime proposal she could have imagined, renting a red Porsche convertible for the weekend and zooming her to a sunny, breeze-swept cliff top overlooking the mouth of the Columbia River before literally dropping to his knees and holding out a huge bunch of flowers and a ring.

He'd worked at their marriage, and had supported her desire for a child all the way. In fact, he'd pushed her harder and faster than she wanted to be pushed over the IVF treatment because he'd known her heart's desire and he wanted her to have it. After batteries of tests, the doctors had found no specific cause for her infertility, and she'd wanted to relax about it, give themselves another six months or even a year to conceive naturally. She'd suggested taking a couple of pampering vacations. "Can't we go easy on ourselves for a bit, and maybe it will happen on its own?"

John had disagreed. "If you want a baby that much, let's do what it takes, let's do it now, let's go with the maximum number of embryos the clinic is willing to implant. Why wait? Why do things by halves? I want to make you happy, Stacey."

Ex-husbands didn't have to be the scum of the earth.

But happiness didn't have to be something a man bulldozed in your direction because he was too impatient and single-minded to wait, said a little voice inside her.

Sometimes John had tried too hard.

"…the classic case of a couple who's trying too hard," she heard Jake say, in answer to someone's question, and wondered how long she had gone without hearing anything of what was being said, before his words had somehow dovetailed with the direction of her own thoughts.

The female half of another couple raised her hand. "This isn't really a question, but I'd just like to say… Dr. Logan, I don't know if you remember us. Mike and Pattie McLeod, from Denver? You helped us to conceive through the GIFT procedure."

He took a closer look, then smiled. "Hey, yes, of course I remember you, Mrs. McLeod."

"Oh, make it Pattie, please!"

"Pattie. Little guy came six weeks early, didn't he? What was his name?"

"Lucas. And we'd lost his twin early in the pregnancy."

"I remember that, too."

"But you were so good, Dr. Logan. We moved to Portland six months ago. Lucas is almost two now, healthy and happy. We wanted to try for another one and we were so happy to hear you were involved with the program at Portland General. If anyone here is undecided about their options, we'd have no hesitation in recommending Dr. Logan, would we, Mike?"

"None," he agreed. "He knows what he's doing, he explains what he's doing and he cares." There was a satisfied murmur from the crowd.

Jake seemed pleased at the positive testimonial, but he didn't dwell on it, Stacey noted.

"The McLeods just mentioned GIFT," he said quickly. "Gamete Intra-Fallopian Transfer. We've already talked about it, but Mike and Pattie, would you be willing to answer people's questions privately when we break for supper? The perspective of anyone who's actually been through these treatments is sometimes more helpful than anything a doctor can say."

Mike McLeod looked to his wife for confirmation, then said, "Sure, we're happy to talk about our experience."

Jake answered several more questions, then Stacey returned to the podium to introduce one of the fertility clinic nurses who outlined the steps a couple could expect to go through, beginning with their initial assessment.

Finally, she introduced Marian Novak, the Director of Adoption Services at Children's Connection. "Because, as Marian will tell you, biological parenthood isn't the only way."

Marian was a powerful advocate for the value of adopting older children or those with special needs, and Stacey saw one couple look at each other and nod, as if they'd been given something new and exciting to consider.

Another couple didn't appear to be so happy. The husband raised his hand and stuck out his jaw. "We heard there'd been some serious problems here a few years ago," he said. "IVF mix-ups, illegal adoption arrangements and even kidnappings? I gotta tell you, those are three of my worst nightmares, and I would sue the butts off of you people if we came to you for treatment and anything went wrong. What can you tell us to convince us those kinds of things can't happen again?"

Before Jake could even turn in her direction, Stacey jumped up.

"I'll take this one," she said, smiling. "Sir, the reason none of that can happen again is because it was the product of a particular, very personal and very greedy vendetta. There were only a couple of people involved and they are out of the picture now. Justice was served, and any mix-ups or illegal dealings have been corrected and resolved. I can assure you, with the full backing of the hospital's legal department, that there will be no risk of any mistakes with fertility treatments or adoption arrangements at Children's Connection in the future."

"Are you prepared to put that in writing?" the man asked.

"It is in writing already, in our brochure," she said firmly, "And elsewhere."

Feeling heat rising inside her clothing, she waited for more of his hostile attitude, not knowing what more she could do. She could see he had genuine concerns, and she understood the reasons for them, but he was the kind of man who expressed anxiety in the form of aggression, and she didn't want to see all of the good work that Jake and Justine and Marian had done this evening unraveled by one critical question.

"We'll think about it," the man growled. "Trust me, we're researching our options down to the last detail, and if there is even a whisper of more trouble, we will go elsewhere."

Jake stepped back to the podium. "As you should, if that's how you feel," he said. "Thanks for asking about it, and thanks for the clarification, Stacey."

When Stacey stood at the podium for the last time, it was simply to thank the speakers and invite everyone to enjoy their supper. Several couples immediately steered in Jake's direction and she had to move quickly to reach him first.

"You're going to be swamped with questions," she warned. "Let me get you something to eat and drink, because you'll never reach the table yourself."

He looked grateful. "Coffee and a couple of chocolate chip cookies?"

"Coming right up. Just milk?"

"Yep, as always. Don't forget Marian and Justine. They're going to be kept busy, also."

She nodded. "But I already know their supper preferences."

"Of course. You've organized these evenings before."

"I enjoy them. People arrive nervous and

skeptical and leave energized, ready to consider options they hadn't even known about before. I really like to see that transition."

"So do I. And it was a great idea to have Marian speak, as well."

"She's like you, fairly new at the Children's Connection and a great asset."

His reply this time was indirect. "Stacey… you must have a sitter at home?"

"That's right. But Max and Ella should be sound asleep, letting her study, so don't feel that you have to hurry the session to a close. Let me get you that supper."

Stacey departed in search of Jake's coffee and cookies before he could say anything further to her. He saw the three couples who were hanging back, awaiting his attention, and stepped toward them, having to work harder than usual to respond to their questions with the right enthusiasm.

He wanted to keep talking to Stacey, follow through on his question about the sitter.

He'd been aware of her all through the evening. The way she'd hopped up so cheerfully from her seat at the end of the front row when it was her turn at the podium. The way she'd folded his jacket and sweater over the back of the chair next to her and smoothed them with her hands. The way she'd encouraged people with their questions, repeating them more loudly or in clearer language when not everyone had heard and understood. One woman had rambled on for too long with no apparent question or point to make, and Stacey had managed to cut her off without any feelings getting hurt.

A week ago, he'd had no thought that he would ever see her again. Now, already, she'd begun to matter, and he knew he'd be left with a sense of loss if they couldn't find the right way to connect. Was she right to say that *amicable* too often meant *superficial?* He had a powerful recognition of her innate worth in his life, and realized in a moment of blinding understanding that he wanted more, much more, than simply their shared memories, both good and bad.

Seconds later, she brought him his refreshments, slipping into a momentary gap when no one was talking to him. "You were very good tonight," she said.

"So were you." He lowered his voice. "You did a great job handling the issue of the incidents that happened three years ago. Thanks for that."

"Part of the job. We've had questions on it in the past, although this was the most direct. I was grateful to you when you moved the subject on, without playing it down too much."

"Well, I would hate to see this place tainted by problems that no longer exist. The public may have a short memory, but if it's jogged by fresh and overemotive coverage in the press…" He stopped, realizing that they were in danger of being overheard.

"Dr. Logan…?" a woman began.

More questions. Before the couple could claim his full attention, he added quickly to Stacey, "It's still early and you have the sitter. Could we go somewhere?"

"More food?"

He shrugged. "The company would be the important part."

Her blue eyes seemed to glisten as she looked at him. He prepared to marshal his arguments.

No strings.

No heavy weight from the past.

Just as friends.

But before he could say another word, she nodded. "Yes. You're right. It would be the company, and I'd like that. I'll call the sitter and tell her I'll be later than I planned."

* * *

They drove in Jake's car to a restaurant-bar that overlooked the Willamette River and a marina of pleasure boats.

The night was mild for early January. The past few days of rain had eased back to a damp mist and the stretch of dark water overlooked by the restaurant appeared like a stage set. There were blue halos around the streetlamps, streaks of fog hovering like transparent fabric behind the dim shapes of the boats, and white fairy lights shaping the bare limbs of the trees.

"Would you like to walk for a bit?" Jake suggested as he shrugged broad shoulders into his jacket. "The air feels good. I was called in for a delivery at five this morning and haven't been out of the hospital since."

"You must be tired! I don't know how doctors deal with the sleep disruption, actually." Stacey unfolded her plum-colored coat and he held it for her. When he stood behind her, she felt the brush of his breath over her hair. "Getting up in the night if Max or Ella has a nightmare is enough for me, now that we're done with night feedings. Of course we can get some air. I'd enjoy it."

They began to walk. Jake linked his arm through Stacey's and she squeezed back, giving him a sideways smile. She was glad she'd said yes to coming out with him tonight. It felt like the first step toward something good—something she could reach and hold and claim if she worked at it hard enough.

"Mmm, this is good," Jake said after several minutes. "It's waking me up. I should get a decent sleep tonight. Somebody else is on call, and I don't have surgery in the morning so I don't start until nine."

Mild for January still meant that the temperature was in the thirties. Their breath steamed, but with the brisk pace he set she was soon warm in her thick wool coat. Warm and content.

"How come babies always seem to come in the early hours of the morning?" she said. "The twins were born at twenty after four. I'm sure my doctor was cursing me."

"Who was your ob-gyn?"

"Damian Cheeley. John knew him from college. I liked him, but I didn't love him."

"I don't know the name."

"He's moved on, now. Somewhere in California, I think."

They were quiet for a few moments, until the chill began to sink into their bones. "Ready to turn around and head inside?" Jake asked.

"Yes, I am, but this was good. I'm glad we didn't go in direct from the car."

Inside, on the upper level at a table by the windows, the aroma of beer and seafood that reached Stacey's nose made a mockery of the instant coffee granules and packet cookies she had prepared for the information night, and Jake confessed that he'd eaten dinner on the run. "Mind if we check out their bar food?"

"Not at all."

After some lighthearted debate, they ordered a mixed platter of appetizers and a light beer each, then forgot how hungry they were as they talked.

"Tell me more about the twins," Jake said. He watched Stacey's face light up at once, but she quickly schooled her expression so that the light dimmed again. He didn't understand why.

"They're good," she said. "I mean, they're great, obviously. They're very different."

Why the awkwardness?

"Tell me," he insisted.

She smiled—the dimpled sarcastic version. "Jake, I have to warn you, I am completely capable of boring people into a hypnotic trance talking about my kids. You were polite enough to ask and now I've answered. Let's leave it, okay? Tell me about, oh, Australia. Did you have kangaroos in your backyard?"

"Yeah, and when I wanted a ride somewhere I just hopped into a pouch and gave directions. Stace, please don't tell me you're avoiding talking about your kids because you think I'm one of those Child Free Zone types who—"

"Child Free Zone?"

"You know what I mean. Drop their friends when the birth announcement arrives. Ask to get moved on airplanes if there's a toddler less than three rows away. I deliver babies for a living, remember? I like them. I just—" He stopped.

No. No. Don't say it.

He didn't want to talk about Anna again. They'd already trodden that ground. It was time to move on, find some new connections…if that was possible.

Their eyes met for a moment—hers looked darker in the dimness of the bar—and he suspected she felt the same as he did. If they couldn't move forward, then they'd soon reach a level where they gave each other awkward smiles when they passed in a hospital corridor, or pretended they hadn't seen each other standing in the cafeteria line at lunch. He didn't want that.

And Stacey…?

"Don't let Anna's loss darken your life this way, Jake," she said on a whisper. "She deserves better than that. She deserves to bring you good things, to warm your heart, not close it off."

"I don't see it that way. And I don't want to talk about it." He gritted his teeth and felt his hands ball into fists. "Seriously, switch topics, can you?"

"If that's what you want." Their food and drinks arrived, but she ignored them and spoke fast, her words a clear attempt to drown the sound of words he didn't want to hear or say. "Max is more timid and clingy than his sister. I think he's going to be musical. But I'm probably kidding myself. He sure hammers away on his little xylophone. So definitely either music or carpentry."

Jake laughed.

"Ella is more confident and outgoing. But she's creative, too. For a two-year-old she can really focus on things like paint and clay. Great fine motor skills." She pushed her fork into a stuffed mushroom and began to relax.

He nodded. "I'm sure they're both bright."

They talked about her life some more, as they ate. Practical details such as the fact that she'd bought out John's half of their house after the divorce. A little about her sister. Giselle had called the other night and left a message, but Stacey hadn't yet called her back and felt guilty about it.

"Except that when we do talk, it's always about how perfect her life is, and what darling gifts Mom gave her for her birthday, and how much Mom adores Stirling—Giselle's husband—and the exquisite work the landscapers did on her new courtyard…. I can't describe our relationship. I'm sounding like a bitch."

"Yeah, you should be the model for a soap opera character, Stace," he drawled. "Your heart is truly black."

She laughed. "Okay, so I'm in such a rut, I can't even cut it as a bitch."

"Didn't I apologize about saying the rut thing?"

"You did, but that doesn't mean I'm going to let it drop. Now it's your turn to talk. Detail on the kangaroos. If they're not as cute as they look in pictures, Logan, I authorize you to lie."

"They're cute, Handley, it's okay." He reached his hand out to hers across the table. "And I think we're okay now, too."

"I think so, yes."

She left her hand where it was, cradled in his, and neither of them spoke for a long time as they ate and drank. Finally, he was the one to break the silence. "Are you…pretty stunned…by how much…?" He broke off, struggling for words. "By just how much is still going on here?"

She nodded, and said everything else with her blue eyes. They dropped to her empty plate after a moment, as if the intensity was too hard to handle. "I should get back to the sitter soon. She's a college freshman and she has classes tomorrow. Can you just excuse me for a moment?"

"Sure."

She slid out of her seat.

Jake looked at his watch. Eleven-thirty. He should be dropping in his tracks after his long day. But Stacey had always energized him. Something about her warm heart and lively mind. In his experience, you didn't always find the two in combination. It definitely energized him. A couple of minutes later, as he watched her coming back from the bathroom with her curves and her grace unconsciously on display, he felt as if he'd dropped fifteen years.

And he'd acquired the hormones to match.

The hormones, and a willingness to plan like a military strategist for the right opportunity to kiss her.

If he kissed her now, across the table, the moment would end in a few seconds. If he waited until he dropped her back at her car, still parked at the hospital, she would be focused on getting home, relieving the sitter, checking on her sleeping kids. But if they walked out of here with their coat sleeves brushing together and he kissed her on the deserted sidewalk…

Moments after they left the restaurant, he stopped beneath a starburst of winter fairy lights and turned her into his arms, knowing it was right.

"Jake?" she murmured, then, "Oh…"

He still knew just how to touch her.

He had taken her by surprise. Which was crazy when Stacy considered the awareness that had crackled between them all evening, both at the information session and in the more intimate atmosphere of the waterfront bar.

He'd picked his moment perfectly. She had just begun to think ahead, hoping Melody would be happy about the extra money she would earn babysitting this late, wondering if there was any chance that Max and Ella would play quietly in their cribs when they awoke in the morning, instead of dragging her out of bed at six.

Now, these thoughts were chased away by

the pressure of his hand and the touch of his mouth. His arms wrapped around her, fitting against her body exactly right. She could feel his strength, the muscles beneath his jacket and sweater, the heat coursing through him.

His mouth felt warm and tasted sweet.

And just *right,* in a way that John's mouth never had.

Why was it so magical? Why did the whole world suddenly make sense because of this?

She gave him everything with her response—honesty and promise and faith. *Yes, I want this. Yes, I'll give you more. Yes, we can make it into something good, I know we can. Taste me, feel the way I open to you, I'm holding nothing back.*

She pressed her breasts against his chest, splayed her fingers on his back and felt his hands drop to cup her backside through her coat and pull her even closer.

"Stacey," he groaned.

"Don't stop." She ran her fingers up through his hair, let her tongue tangle with his, rocked her hips deliberately against his arousal, its hard bulk making her soften and swell even further. Even through their clothing she had that same intensely physical sense that they fit, that they belonged. That if they went further it would only get better.

"Do you know what you're doing to me?" Jake asked in a hushed whisper.

"Yes."

"Do it some more."

"Oh, yes…"

He only broke from their kiss because someone walked by, their footsteps cracking out like warning gunfire. Even now, his mouth was only a few inches away, his eyes close enough to drown in. "Can we see each other on the weekend?"

Totally shaken, she pulled back a little farther and tried to lighten the atmosphere. "I don't know. Does this still fall within your definition of amicable?"

"Uh, no, I guess it's gone up a couple of notches from there."

She nodded.

"You haven't answered my question," he prompted her.

"The weekend," she echoed, thoughts all over the place, body aflame.

"I'm not on call." He sounded as vague as she felt. His eyes stayed fixed on her face and his thumb brushed her lower lip. He looked at her mouth, and the look was as powerful as any kiss.

"Right."

"Come over for lunch. You know the address. We'll take it from there."

Take it where?

She didn't dare to ask, because she knew what answer he would give, and once he'd made it explicit and out in the open she would have to stop pretending to herself that this was safe. That she was in control.

She wasn't in control of anything where Jake Logan was concerned. She never had been.

"Sounds good," she managed to say.

"Make it eleven? Later, if you want."

"Eleven will be fine." She could talk to Melody tonight and find out if she was available Saturday. Or maybe her friend, Valbona, would have the twins at her place for a few hours.

Today was Tuesday. Saturday was four days away.

It seemed like too long to wait.

Chapter Five

"Jake?"

"Stacey, don't tell me you're lost," he teased her.

She sounded a little frazzled over the phone, and he had a very selfish plea surging up from inside him which he managed not to voice out loud: Please don't tell me something's come up and you have to cancel.

He'd planned this lunch carefully.

He'd bought cheese sticks, blackberry and apple juice boxes, oven-bake frozen chicken nuggets and fries for the twins, as well as big people food. He'd even gone to the mall this morning and tracked down a toy store. There was now a big box of brand-new colored plastic building blocks reposing in the center of his abstract-patterned, handwoven great room rug, as well as a couple of other toddler playthings he'd borrowed yesterday from his new nurse-receptionist at the clinic. He liked the color and promise they created.

"I'm not lost," Stacey said. "But I think I'm going to have to cancel. My sitter just called, three minutes ago. She's sprained her ankle. So she says. I mean, she's usually pretty reliable, but at the moment I could kill her if she's making it up just because she doesn't feel like coming out in the rain. I'm going to be brutally honest, Jake, I've really been looking forward to this, and now…"

She sounded close to tears.

Or violence.

Which pretty much summed up his own reaction.

"You're supposed to bring the twins, Stace."

"I am?" She sounded blank and astonished.

"We went through this, didn't we? I'm not a Child Free Zone. I assumed they'd be coming. I've catered for them. Plastic blocks and juice boxes."

She sniffed the tears back and he heard a

smile creep into her voice. "They don't eat plastic blocks. Too spicy. Especially the red ones."

Nope, sorry, he wasn't going to laugh. He was actually angry that she thought he hadn't planned on including her kids.

He waited.

"Jake, you didn't have to do this," she finished after a moment.

"No?" he drawled. "Thanks for pointing that out. I thought it was a court-ordered requirement. My mistake."

"Why are you mad?"

"Because of your assumptions. Which, as far as I'm concerned, we've already addressed."

There was a moment's silence as she considered this, then she said crisply, "I think you're wrong. But we can debate it over lunch. I'm glad you were expecting Max and Ella. We'll be a little late because I have to get them ready. But we'll be there."

He was still angry forty minutes later, when she and the twins arrived. The rain had temporarily eased back to low cloud and his breath steamed as he stepped into the driveway to meet them. Stacey smiled and said hi and bundled the twins out of the car, then opened the trunk to retrieve a bulging diaper bag, a portable crib and a covered dish.

She wore a very feminine version of a leather bomber jacket, as well as jeans and a fuzzy sweater in bright sky blue. The dark brown boots beneath the jeans gave Jake flashes of X-rated fantasy, the way their heels snapped on the cement.

"Are we still mad at each other?" she said, while Max and Ella rushed over to the browned winter grass and started inspecting wet leaves.

"Let's explore that."

She sighed. "Obviously we are. Jake, you invited me to lunch, you didn't specifically say to bring the kids, and you're a single man with a beautiful home. I don't think my assumptions were an insult, the way you seem to feel."

He held his ground. "If I hadn't wanted the twins, I would have suggested dinner at a fancy restaurant."

"I'll remember that next time."

"Why are *you* angry?" he asked.

"Because I don't think you have a right to be."

"I think I do. You keep doing this. You've put me in a box labeled People Not To Share My Kids With, and I've already told you it's not where I want to be. I do have the right to be angry."

She looked sideways at him, and said in a measured way, "You seriously want me to share my kids with you?"

"Yes!"

"Logan, you have no clue what you're in for!" She grinned at him, like sun coming out from behind the clouds, and suddenly everything felt good again.

"Swings!" Ella said, at that moment. She'd glimpsed the sturdy wooden swing and slide set in his back garden, a legacy of the previous owners, who'd been sent to Europe for a couple of years for work and who had kids. Ella headed toward it, Max right on her heels.

Jake was impressed at their speed. He swung the diaper bag onto his shoulder, picked up the portable crib by its handle and started for the house, but found Stacey's dish thrust into his spare hand a moment later. He had to stop to adjust the diaper bag and the crib so he could manage it all. Stacey had already set off after the twins.

He watched her and soon saw why. Ella reached the swing set before Max and launched herself, stomach first, onto the belt-shaped rubber seat. She overshot the distance and her head hit the grass. Loud crying started. Stacey scooped her up and began to soothe her by bouncing her on one hip, while simultaneously stopping the crooked motion of the swing from knocking Max over on the rebound.

Jake began to think that Stacey might be right.

He had no clue what he was in for.

He couldn't believe how fast the two-year-olds had gotten into trouble, nor how soon Stacey had seen it coming. He dumped the bag and the dish in the house, came through the back door and found relative tranquility at the swing set. Stacey pushed Ella on the rubber swing with one hand and Max on the plastic one with the other.

"Is she okay?" he asked.

"It's always a good sign when they cry like that, right away."

"Yeah?"

"If they're seriously hurt, they cry different or they don't cry at all. Ella is the queen of really yelling when she gets a bump, and then forgetting all about it thirty seconds later."

"She certainly looks fine now."

"She is. Apart from the grass stain on her forehead."

"Actually, I thought that was a good look for her."

"Oh, please. You can push Max, if you want."

She grinned at him. "It's incredibly b-o-r-i-n-g after about three minutes."

"You're not supposed to say that, are you?"

"I know I'm not. So I didn't. I spelled it."

He pressed the issue, sounding deliberately dense because he wanted to dig a little deeper into who Stacey-the-Mom really was. What had she said the other night? That Anna deserved better than to darken his life and should warm his heart instead. He couldn't see it. How did Stacey manage all the contradictions in being a parent?

"It's meant to be very fulfilling, this kind of thing, isn't it?" It felt like dangerous territory, yet necessary. "Quality time with kids."

"You mean because Hollywood actresses with their fleets of nannies always say so?"

"That's where I get most of my information on parenting. From Hollywood actresses."

"Seriously? I mean, not the where you get your information thing, but do you want my serious answer?"

"Yes. I do."

"It *is* fulfilling. It *is* quality time. We're out in the fresh air. They're happy. I'm getting an upper body workout. I know I'm doing the right thing as a parent. It can be frustrating, too, sometimes, like if I try to come around to face them and push them from the front because then we can smile at each other and I love that. But they always tell me—Ella's the ringleader on this—'Back! Back!' I guess to create a better illusion that she's flying free? So there I am, standing behind them, push-two-three-four, push-two-three-four, Max, Ella, Max, Ella, like a machine, for twenty minutes at a stretch."

"You could say, we've had enough swinging for now, guys, let's do something else."

"And then what? There are twelve waking toddler twin hours in every day, and every one of them has to be filled with something that's not dangerous or going to get chocolate or paint on my carpet. Do you want total honesty, here, Jake, or a sanitized version?"

"Total. Always, from you." He dropped his voice and saw her instinctive glance in his direction. Their eyes met and communicated too much.

Too much instinctive understanding.

Too much connection.

The dishonesty of his breakup with her seventeen years ago was a mistake he'd been too immature to avoid back then, but he vowed not to repeat it now.

The moment rattled him and he looked away.

"Total, Jake?" Stacey said. "Okay. As a

nearly full-time single parent, you learn to be grateful for merely being bored."

"Instead of…?"

"Completely exhausted and at your wits' end and in need of therapy."

"Stace, I thought you loved this. You said the other night—"

"I do. I love it down to my toes. I am so nuts about these guys I would crawl on my hands and knees licking broken glass for the sake of their well-being and happiness. But I've discovered that I can be incredibly fulfilled in the abstract and yet frequently bored and frustrated in the day-to-day moments."

"You wouldn't think of increasing your work hours to get more of that kind of fulfillment? Professional, out in the world, with other adults. You told me there's the option of expanding your job into full-time if you want."

"Not until they're in school. I guess I'm old-fashioned. Two days a week is enough when they're this small."

"Why? If they enjoy the day-care center, what's the problem?"

"It's not that simple. They enjoy it sixteen hours a week. I'm not convinced forty or more would be good for them."

"So make it simple for me."

"Simple," she echoed. "Okay." She took a breath. "I just happen to believe, even though it's not always convenient or easy to believe it, and even though a lot of people would argue differently, that children under the age of five deserve to spend most of their waking hours in the care of someone who loves them. I don't think it matters if that person is a parent or a grandparent or a family friend or if it's a mix of two or three people, or what, and I know it's not a possibility for some people—I'm so lucky that John's job means he can afford to help finance this for us—but I think in an ideal world, it's what every kid would have."

"And you stick to that idea, even when you're b-o-r-e-d?"

"Yep."

"Huh."

"What?"

"Nothing. I'm just thinking."

"So I stand on my soapbox and spill my entire child-care philosophy, and you get to say nothing and just think?"

"You're a very interesting person, Stacey."

"Although stuck in a rut."

"You really don't let things go, sometimes, do you?"

"Nope." She grinned. "And, now, see, we're

not bored—I like it when I'm at the playground with other carers and we get talking—and the twins are extremely happy with our push-two-three-four rhythm, so there's always a bright side. Oh, speaking of bright sides, that's an apple cake I brought for lunch. One of their favorites."

"Insurance against a mealtime battle?"

"Something like that."

They pushed the swings in silence for a while. Push-two-three-four. Push-two-three-four. Max and Ella. Ella and Max. Jake saw Stacey's point. B-o-r-i-n-g. And yet at the same time...good. Really good.

A low cloud of fog hung in the trees, which dripped with silvery water. The damp air magnified the fresh, pungent scent of pine needles, and somebody nearby must have a wood fire burning in their home because he could smell the smoke. Wearing a jacket and leather gloves, he was warm even without a hat, and the bite of the cold against his ears was strangely pleasant.

The twins were so cute, in colorful down jackets that turned their little bodies into soft, bulky packages. They had red pom-pom hats and matching mittens and probably red noses, too, although he couldn't see their faces right now.

"My arms are starting to ache," Stacey announced, after some minutes more. "Guys, want to get down and explore? Wanna try the slide?" She nudged Ella the short distance to the ground, which made Max at once begin to squirm. His swing was higher, with a safety chain across the front, so he needed extra help.

Jake tried to lift him, but the little boy caught one foot in the leg hole of the plastic swing and they both got stuck. Should he try to pull Max up or push him back down? How come the kid's legs didn't seem to have knees? How come Jake could rotate an unborn baby inside its mother's belly, or free a stuck shoulder halfway through a birth, but he couldn't get a two-year-old out of a swing? "Uh, Stacey…?"

"I know. He's still learning to work out when to bend. Let me do it."

"Would they be getting hungry?" he asked, while she deftly folded and pulled her child in the right places, got him free of the swing and down to the ground. "I should go inside and start up those nuggets."

"You're confident we've got that oven control system down, now?"

"I practiced the whole of Sunday."

She laughed, and he felt an insane spurt of pleasure and warmth.

He went ahead of her and the twins. He put nuggets and fries in the oven and the deli soup he'd purchased into a pot on the stove. He set out bread, cold meat, cheese, juice boxes and several other items on the kitchen table.

By this time he'd expected to hear Stacey and the children entering the house but there was no sign of them, so he went out through the back door and found them still making their slow progress toward the back door. Apparently the details of his yard were a lot more fascinating to young eyes and young fingers than he'd realized.

Stacey seemed impressed, also. She had that healthy outdoor pink to her cheeks and her eyes were bright. Her nose matched her kids' noses, which almost matched the red of their hats but not quite. "You have quite a piece of land!"

"I was told it's over an acre. A big part of why I rented the place, actually. I'd gotten tired of high-rise apartments. There's a sense of space here, neighbors aren't too close, and there are some great trails through the woods nearby. I'd like to cycle when the weather gets warmer, or do some cross-country skiing if we get snow."

"And that's still your ground beyond the holly hedge?" She pointed in that direction, then looked at the twins to check what they were doing.

"Yes, there's a pool back there," Jake told her. "You can't see it because of the vegetation."

"Is it covered and fenced?"

"Uh, yeah, but I'm not sure if the gate is locked."

"Hopefully it has a childproof catch."

"I'll check it, if they want to play outside again."

"Thanks. I'd never let them outside on their own at this age, but with these guys there's no such thing as being too careful."

"Are you ready to come in?"

"I've been ready for ten minutes." She smiled. "But some of us are exploring."

"So I noticed. They won't eat those berries, will they?"

"They've been told."

"Is that enough?"

"They're a lot better about that kind of thing than they were six months ago. 'Tastes yucky,' should be good enough."

"And there are mushrooms growing on a couple of the trees that wouldn't be safe to eat, either."

"I'll watch out for those, too, then."

"Good. Um, let's think, is there anything else?"

Looking around in case more warnings were needed, he discovered that his entire spacious, relaxing, woodsy yard had suddenly become a death trap. Swings that could bump heads, poisonous berries and fungus, the treachery of the swimming pool, an unlocked hatch leading to the space beneath the house, where the owners had helpfully left toxic lawn care chemicals and wasp spray…

The list went on.

No wonder Stacey kept checking on the kids, didn't let them out of her sight for a second and always stayed a scant three steps behind. Right now, in the middle of him saying he hoped she still liked cream of mushroom soup, she told Ella quickly, "Sweetheart, not the berries, remember? They're pretty in your hand but, eww, very, very yucky taste, okay? All bitter. We'll put them down and wash—"

She stopped.

Too late.

Ella had squeezed her fists around the berries to see what a lovely goo they made. And it was indeed lovely—all red and orange and smooshy in her palm and between her fingers. She looked up, wrinkling her nose and grinning.

"—your hands," Stacey finished weakly, and just managed to lunge forward and grab Max's hands before he did the same thing. She shook the berries from his hands, saying, "Look! It's raining pretty berries, Max, isn't that great?" She added without a pause, "I love cream of mushroom soup. Which bathroom should I use for this?"

"When do you sit down?" Jake asked, quite appalled. "Um, there's a powder room…"

"When my legs give out from under me." He saw the dimple in her cheek as she smiled. She could tell how he felt, and she seemed to think it was pretty funny. "This way to the powder room? Thanks."

She held Ella's hands carefully at the wrists. Envisaging a new smooshy red and orange decorative wall treatment on top of his rented paintwork, Jake was grateful for her dexterity and foresight. He held open the back door for her and she frowned at him as she passed. "Are you okay, Jake? No, Ella, sweetheart, I'm not letting go of your hands till we get to the powder room. Is it heated up already?"

"The powder room?"

"The soup."

"I'm fine. Keeping up two entirely separate conversation threads at the same time is more challenging than I'd expected, however."

"Actually, I think we have three going, right now."

He counted. Soup, hands and how Stacey managed to sit down. She was right.

Good grief, he was an obstetrician. He brought babies into the world every day of the week. Sometimes older siblings came in with their mothers for prenatal appointments. His offices, in various cities around the world, had always featured sturdy toys in the waiting area, and he'd witnessed his share of tantrums and curious fingers and misbehavior.

But he hadn't actually spent any of his leisure time around kids, and definitely not twins. Two-year-old, lively, curious, strong-willed twins, whose mother had arrowed her way straight back into his heart after seventeen years as if she could have found her way there blindfolded.

He felt dizzy.

Stacey and the twins came as a package deal. He would have to be pretty dumb not to understand this at first glance. He thought he had already understood it. He'd been angry at her, less than an hour ago, for questioning his willingness to include her kids in his life. Now he realized that his thinking hadn't even scraped the surface.

If he and Stacey were going to have anything more than the most casual—*amicable*—of professional friendships while he stayed in Portland, he'd have to make some kind of a commitment to Ella and Max—at the very least a commitment to keeping a safe watch over them while he was in their company, and to considering their needs and their limitations when he planned time spent with their mother.

What if he started to care about them?

Or what if he didn't?

He didn't know which possibility scared him more.

As Stacey trundled Ella into the powder room with her messy little hands stretched out in front of her and Max following close behind, he heard a loud, spluttering hiss from the kitchen. The cream of mushroom soup had just boiled over on the stove.

"Put the straw in your mouth, and then I'll poke it through the hole, Max. Jake, no, don't let her do it herself, because they always—"

Stacey stopped.

Too late.

Again.

Ella had pushed the juice box straw through the foil circle at the top, unconsciously squeezing the box as she did so. Since she didn't have the straw in her mouth the way Max did, the juice box immediately became a fountain, squirting a spurt of sticky liquid all over the table. Stacey had learned about this phenomenon the hard way. "Sorry, Jake."

"It's fine." He grabbed a handful of napkins and mopped up the mess. "I don't think we have quite all of it spilled on the table," he drawled. "Maybe she could squeeze harder next time."

Stacey knew he couldn't possibly consider this a relaxing meal, and yet she did.

He'd done a good job. Everything was already set out on the table when they sat down, so she didn't need to keep jumping up in search of ketchup or napkins or spoons, the way she had had to do during her most recent spectacularly unsuccessful visit with the twins to her parents in San Diego, over Christmas.

And so far no one had cried, no one had refused to eat, no one had discovered any inventive and messy new uses for their lunch—oh, except Ella with the juice, and that was an accident.

With nuggets and fries, juice and grapes all going down nicely, Stacey relaxed and began to eat her soup, with crusty pieces of bread on the side.

This little dining alcove set in a bay window that opened from the kitchen was a great place for family eating. With the rainy days and dull skies of winter in this part of the country, even native Portlanders could crave extra light in January. The large, double-glazed windowpanes on three sides of the dining alcove almost made her feel as if the four of them were eating outdoors, and the warm air coming up through the floor vents kept everything cozy. The twins' noses weren't pink anymore. Her own ears had warmed.

She saw a couple of gray squirrels chasing each other across the grass and around a tree trunk with their fluffy tails rippling. The sun broke briefly through the cloud cover, making the wet trees glisten and the grass steam.

"This is great, Jake. I love your house."

"Thanks. I'm actually not thrilled with the decorating, but I can't work out why. Have some cheese. The ham is really good, too."

"I think it's too coordinated. Yes, please cut me a piece of that one, and excuse me for reaching across."

"Too coordinated? By the way, I think I'm getting the hang of the two conversations at once thing."

"Max, honey, let's keep your sleeve out of the ketchup." She looked at her son, then back at Jake. "You're doing great with it. It's verbal multitasking. Men aren't supposed to be good at it. I guess because it was done professionally, all in one swoop."

"Swoop is right. She descended, she decided, she decorated, she left."

"You need a few things that don't fit. That's great, Ella. It's empty now, put it down, that's right. You didn't pick up anything during your travels? Tribal art, or landscape photographs? No knickknacks passed down from your grandparents?"

"I've resisted that sort of thing."

"No moss gathering. The original rolling stone."

"Did you want beer or wine, by the way?"

"At lunch? Fatal! Makes me too sleepy, and the worst thing is if I ever nap along with the twins. I feel off-line for the rest of the day."

"I wouldn't call myself a rolling stone."

She gave him a crooked smile. "But if you did, which one would it be? Mick Jagger? Keith Richards? Or Charlie Watts?"

He sat back and laughed.

Definitely a relaxing meal.

Afterward, she offered to clean up and he took the twins into the great room where they were delighted to discover the huge, brand-new tub of blocks, which were big and chunky and exactly right for their little fingers. She could hear the three of them through the open doorway as she wiped down the table and stacked the dishwasher.

"Ship? Shall we make a ship now? Great tower, Max. Way to go, Ella! Knocking it over! Oh, Max, you're not happy about that? Hey, little guy, no big deal, look, we'll build it up again."

When she'd finished in the kitchen, she couldn't stop herself from creeping to listen and look without announcing her presence. Jake was on his denim-clad knees on the elegant handwoven rug, his eyes narrowed and the tip of his tongue escaping between his lips as he pushed each block into place. He had his gray sweater pushed to his elbows and a lick of hair out of place.

Max trotted to and fro, providing further raw material for an already enormous, wobbly, multitiered construction. Meanwhile, Ella did her own thing with great concentration a few feet away, and Jake found time to make comments and suggestions that kept her interest high.

"Okay, now here comes the storm," Jake said. "Are you going to be the storm with me,

Max, are you going to be the wind? We're going to see if we can blow it down without even touching it. Man, it's wobbly enough, I don't think we're going to have a problem. Okay, ready? Blow!"

They both blew with all their might and the towers swayed and toppled and scattered noisily across the rug. Jake sat back on his heels and went, "Woo-*hoo!*" He grinned and slapped his palms against his strong thighs.

Max jumped up and down and clapped his hands and howled with happiness. It was gorgeous, but he would *never* settle down enough for his nap if Jake kept this up, and when Max didn't nap he was a miserable, tantrum-prone mess by five o'clock and he dragged his sister into the emotional vortex along with him, so…

"Wow!" Stacey said, coming forward, wondering how she was going to handle this.

Her heart gave a sudden twist.

Jake had been so great today.

Really, seriously, great.

He'd thought about the twins' needs in advance. He'd dealt with the chaos and mess they inevitably generated, and had laughed about it. He'd even managed to carry through that whole if-you-were-a-famous-music-star-who-would-it-be conversation to the point where she'd admitted to a secret and pretty implausible affinity with all three Dixie Chicks.

"You sing their songs in the shower?"

Yes. She did.

But she still couldn't let Jake unknowingly sabotage Max's nap.

"What a great storm!" she finished when she reached them. "You flattened the whole block city."

"We're guys," Jake said. "We like a little destruction along with our creativity." He grinned, pleased with himself. His green eyes glinted with a hint of wickedness, inviting her to grin back, arrowing their charm deep inside her.

Her heart shifted again.

Max was already gathering up the blocks, making bulldozer noises, eager to do it all over again.

Maybe she just had to play this straight.

"Can we start to bring it down a little bit, energywise?" she asked Jake quietly. "Naps, you see…"

"Oh, right, of course."

"I mean, occasionally they skip them, but it makes the end of the day—"

"Trust me, Stace, I have no desire for them

to skip their naps. I was hoping to tire them out so they'd take nice long ones."

"Kind of doesn't work that way."

"No?"

"You have to bore them after lunch. Bore and soothe and quiet..." She made spreading motions with her hands, as if calming the wild seas of toddler twin energy.

"Hmm, big mistake with the fun, destructive tower stuff, then."

"We'll work with it. It'll take a little longer, that's all." She began to tidy the blocks into different colored piles, turning the task into a gentle game. Max and Ella grew more attentive and sat down to watch. Twenty minutes later, they began to yawn.

Stacey changed their diapers and set up the portable crib in a spare bedroom. The twins still liked to share it, even though there was barely enough space. She didn't darken the room, but left each child with a book to look at, knowing that they'd eventually lie down, let the books fall onto the sheet beside them and close their eyes.

She told them, "Have a yummy, sleepy rest, now, my two honeys."

Then she went slowly and quietly out of the room. She knew from experience that it was fatal to betray any impatience at this point. If the twins somehow sensed just how much she craved some one-on-one adult company— adult, male, Jake Logan–type company, right now, to be honest—after being with them solidly since six this morning, they might easily decide that napping would mean missing some fun, and ten minutes from now they'd start to cry, louder and louder, until she returned.

There were a couple of days recently when *she'd* cried because they hadn't napped, and on those occasions she hadn't even had Jake waiting for her, with all the promise she'd seen in his eyes today.

She wanted the fulfillment of that promise.

Best to be honest with herself about it. She just *wanted* him. She wanted the sensual magic of their connection, the rightness of his body pressed against hers, the sweet secret she saw in his eyes when they looked at each other up close, the touch of his mouth, even deeper than outside the restaurant on Tuesday night.

She wanted time itself to stop, and the whole world to shrink to a cocoon surrounding herself and Jake, so that all she had to think about was him, their two bodies, their two hearts.

And since the twins would nap at most for ninety minutes, she couldn't afford to wait.

She told him at the foot of the stairs, "I think we're going to be okay with napping. And thank you."

"For what?"

"For trying so hard today."

"But failing miserably?"

"No, no, for doing such a good job with it all, I meant."

"Not convinced that I was especially wonderful, if you want the truth."

"No, really. Some people have no idea of the reality of kids at this age."

She teetered on the edge of telling him that he was better than John—that John sometimes expected too much from two-year-olds, wanted the kind of control and consistency he experienced in his work, and usually yelled in an attempt to get it—but even though they were divorced she tried not to betray that kind of disloyalty toward her ex. After all, he was the twins' father, and always would be.

After a moment of hesitation, she pressed her lips together and said nothing.

Chapter Six

Jake saw the movement of Stacey's mouth and wondered what was on her mind.

Wondered if maybe she'd read *his* mind too clearly.

She'd thanked him for doing a good job, and he thought that he sincerely had, but it was a drop in the ocean. A couple of hours of being good-humored about squished berries and spilled juice, of making the effort to push swings and build towers, of putting the needs of two small children ahead of his own...

It hardly added up to any kind of commitment.

He was left with exactly the same fears as he'd had before.

If he started to care too much about Stacey and her kids, he would feel—and be—as vulnerable as a patient on an operating table in the middle of surgery. If he couldn't manage to care about Max and Ella enough, then they would become an irritating, impossible drag on the relationship, a cause of conflict and dishonesty and mess that would be even worse than what he and Stacey had gone through when Anna had died.

He couldn't see any middle ground.

Meanwhile, here was Stacey, mouth still pressed shut, blue eyes big and wide and jewellike as she looked up at him, the slow beginning of her million-watt smile creeping into her face, and he wanted her so much—just *enjoyed* her so much, everything about her, her humor, her warmth, her courage, her sexy body, the things he'd always enjoyed about her but that seemed so much richer in her now—that he simply didn't have the resolve to push her away, the way he knew he should.

He was the scum of the earth.

Look it in the face, Logan.

He was pond slime.

He was going to kiss her right now, take her

to bed within the next week or two if he could, and pretend to himself that he hadn't even noticed the looming emotional disaster zone lying ahead.

"Oh, hell, Stace," he muttered as he stepped toward her.

She met him halfway, sighing her body into his arms, holding his face between her hands, initiating the kiss more than he did, with her sweet mouth. She closed her eyes, and so did he. He wanted her to sweep him away so that he wasn't fully responsible for any of this. He wanted to know in his heart that, whatever happened, she could never truthfully say that he'd pushed too hard.

She covered his mouth with her soft, full lips and kept her hands in place against his jaw, making their kiss into a prison that felt like heaven. He tried to take control, but she wouldn't let him and he loved every second of her purposeful, teasing dominance. With slow, sensual deliberation, she backed him against the wall at the foot of the stairs and pushed even closer, anchoring his groin against her hips.

They kissed for a long time.

It was glorious.

Fabulous.

Hot.

"I needed this," she whispered at last.

"Me, too."

"Good…"

"Very good." He deepened the kiss again, using his tongue to draw an even fuller response from her.

"…because I need more."

Who had the initiative now? Who was pushing this faster and further? He couldn't have said. He let his shoulder blades loll against the wall and his hips push forward a little, his increasing arousal coexisting with a delicious sense of laziness and a huge appreciation of her feline assertiveness.

He hadn't yet used his hands. They fell to his sides, while his total focus narrowed to the sweet contact of mouth on mouth. When she dragged her lips away, he wanted them back, kept his eyes shut, kept his mouth open a little and waited and just *wanted* her.

"Jake?" For the first time, she sounded tentative. "Touch me?"

He was a total mess, and he'd lost all power to think. "Where?"

"Wherever you want." She took her hands away from his face, gripped his wrists and brought his arms around behind her, planting them on her rear. "I just need to know…that this is coming from you as much as from me."

"How can you even ask? It's you. It's me. I don't even know where you finish and I begin, anymore."

"Prove it," she whispered. "Prove it to me, Jake…"

The need for action surged into him at last. He caressed the two soft curves of her cheeks, found the creases at the tops of her thighs, slid his fingers in closer together. His arousal was packed in tight and hard and large against the front of his jeans. She liked it. She touched him through the cloth, teasing him, smiling while they still kissed, then slid her hand away so that the tips of her fingers brushed his aching, impatient hardness.

"Thank you," she said again. Breathed, rather than said.

"Will you stop that?" he whispered.

"Thanking you? Or…?"

"Yes. Thanking me. Arousing me, definitely do *not* stop that!"

"No? Okay…"

"What are the thanks for, this time? Can I ask?"

"For this. For kissing me. Wanting to kiss me. As much as I want to kiss you."

"Wanting it more."

"Oh, no. Not more…" She ran her fingers through his hair, rocked her hips to and fro across the painful bulk of his erection, pushed her softly rounded breasts into his chest. Did she realize there'd be no stopping them, soon?

She was a grown woman, not a naive young girl.

She had to want this as much as he did, or else she was playing with fire.

Meanwhile, he'd already gotten burned. Seriously, if she was going to put the brakes on, she had to do it now or never, and he had to make it clear to her. With aching reluctance, he pulled his mouth away, brushed his nose against hers—oh hell, he was throbbing, he just wanted to keep kissing her…

"Who are you and what have you done with the real Stacey?" he muttered. "I mean, I love this, but—"

"This is me, Jake." She sounded more than a little shaky, and her hand was unsteady, lightly stroking his cheek.

"You claim."

"It's definitely me." She seemed wobbly on her feet, leaning against his whole length to shore herself up.

"Are you sure that this new you is fully aware of what she's doing, and how far it's going to go?"

"I—I admit, I hadn't intended it when I woke

up this morning—" She looked into his eyes, frowning a little. Her mouth looked swollen and her jaw was pink from the rasp of his stubble, even though he'd shaved less than eight hours ago.

"Or even when you came down the stairs?" he suggested.

"I think I half intended it when I came down the stairs. I knew what would happen, what I would want, once we kissed. And I made damned sure that we kissed, so…"

"How much do you intend it now?"

"All the way. I need it. I want it. With you. It's been a long time, and—" She bit her lip. "With you, Jake Logan," she repeated, as if there were no other man in the world.

Elation surged in him, along with his need. He'd begun to shake, too, his knees as weak as hers were. He wanted to squeeze her until she laughed and begged for a chance to breathe. "I'm not going to say, 'Are you sure?' anymore, Stace, because you've had your chance."

"No. This is my chance," she whispered. "When we go back up the stairs, that'll be my chance, and I can't wait."

"Now?"

"Please!"

They went, touching each other all the way.

* * *

There was a gratifying silence upstairs.

Stacey didn't let herself think about the twins asleep behind the closed spare room door. She thought of the other bedroom instead—the big one at the end of the corridor, with its high, wood-beamed ceiling, king-size bed covered in a puffy dark green comforter, and invitingly gaping door.

She wanted this, and she was going into it with her eyes wide-open.

She didn't know where it would lead. There could very easily be a broken heart at the end of it—hers, of course—but she knew it could never be classed as a one-night stand.

Not with Jake Logan.

They reached the bedroom and there was no slow, seductive teasing, just hunger and impatience and need. He swung her around, breathed a hot, moist kiss onto her ear and whispered, "Raise your arms." Helplessly, she did. His knuckles brushed her sensitive sides as he peeled her sweater off, taking with it the snug-fitting black cotton tank she wore beneath.

Before she could react, he cupped his hands over her breasts, and even through the lace cups of her bra, she could feel their heat and their familiarity. Jake's hands. Jake's magic hands. "Oh, Stacey, oh, I want this!" he said.

She let out a sound that was half gasp, half moan, and closed her eyes, then felt him reach around and unfasten her bra. It slipped from her shoulders, brushed her nipples, then fell. He cupped her again, skin to skin this time, and bent to press his mouth to each hardened nipple in turn, like a kiss of greeting. Every nerve ending in her body tightened and sang.

But he wasn't yet content. She heard fabric sliding across skin and opened her eyes again to discover him tossing his sweater onto the floor, reaching for his T-shirt, tossing that, too.

Oh, she'd forgotten that his body looked this good, had forgotten the natural olive tone in his skin that seemed to defy all of winter's attempts to fade it, had forgotten the shading of hair across the muscles of his chest. They stood shamelessly looking at each other, and she knew how much he liked what he saw. The knowledge built her own pleasure higher, and already she felt achingly ready for him.

He held her again, his chest warm and hard against her body. She wrapped her arms tight because it didn't seem that she could ever get enough of him. Even this wasn't close enough.

Even when he kissed her deeply, drowning her mouth with his, it wasn't enough.

He unfastened her jeans and she helped him slide them down over her hips, then remembered aloud, "I'm wearing boots."

"Very sexy boots," he growled. "Sit on the bed." He bent low and slid them from her feet one at a time, along with the silky-thin socks she wore beneath. He curved his warm palms around each bare instep and pressed his lips to her ankles, pulled off her jeans and panties, kissed the tender skin in the crooks of her knees.

Then he moved higher.

She leaned back on her hands, gasping. Her hair fell across her face like a caress. He held her hips as if he thought she might pull away, but she was chained in place by the ecstasy of what he did to her. When she dropped back to the bed, he slid all the way up her body, his chest brushing her breasts, his thighs heavy over hers.

He buried his face in the soft quilt above her shoulder, and then in her hair. She was throbbing, aching with satisfaction and yet ready for more. "Please…" she begged him.

"Not yet. We can make it better." He rolled until she lay on top of him. "You see, I need these." He cupped her breasts again, took them into his mouth, lavished them with erotic sensation until she almost sobbed. "Let me inside you, now," he said at last.

"Oh, please!"

He turned away for a moment and she heard the sound of tearing, bringing her a dose of reality. She'd almost forgotten about the need for such things, and was grateful that he'd thought to protect her. Then again, he wasn't an impulsive teenager anymore. Not emotionally, and not physically. He was mature and sure of himself in every way.

With one hard, sliding motion, he filled her completely, sensitizing her swollen folds to bursting point. She rocked slowly against him over and over, her movement like a ripple through water, her soft lower belly locked seamlessly with his flat expanse of muscle.

By now they barely needed to move. They couldn't move. It all happened without effort or will or impulse. It flooded forward like a torrent, out of their control. He gripped the tops of her thighs with his hands and made one final surging movement and they both cascaded into their release, crying out in unison.

Stacey couldn't speak. No words felt right. After they'd slid apart, she lay with her head pillowed on Jake's chest and just listened to his heartbeat and his breathing, feeling his warm arms around her. She didn't want him to speak—didn't want to have to move or change or think.

Maybe he didn't want to do any of those things, either. He stayed as silent and motionless as she was, waiting for the world to end.

But it kept going, of course.

The numbers on his clock changed, and changed, and changed again. A car went past outside. The soft winter light spilling through the big windows faded into a premature gloom. The clouds had lowered again, and the rain had started. The room was so quiet that Stacey could hear the droplets spitting gently on the glass. It was over an hour since she'd left the twins to fall asleep. They could awaken again at any time.

She envisioned scrambling to get dressed while they stood in their crib, crying and trying to climb out. Ella had made some pretty serious attempts at it lately, gripping the padded rail and stretching her leg up like a mini ballerina. Soon she would succeed, and Max would follow, and one or both of them would topple to the other side and bump their heads hard on the floor.

"Jake…?"

"Beautiful," he murmured, and squeezed her tight. "Oh, Stacey, it was incredible. My heart's still beating too fast."

She couldn't move yet. She had to hold on to this for a little longer.

She reached out her fingers and traced the smooth line of his lips, the skin around his eyes, his neat ears, his hairline, relearning all the familiar things and exploring the new ones— those fine smile wrinkles, the strands of silver-gray. "Yes, it was incredible," she echoed.

"What happens when the twins wake up?"

"I'm hoping to be dressed by then."

"No, but... Do you have to leave?"

"How long do you want us to stay?"

"All night."

Her heart sank as reality rushed in.

They couldn't stay all night.

On the weekends when he didn't see Max and Ella, John always phoned to wish them good-night, and the twins had just recently begun to expect it and enjoy it. They took turns holding the phone to their ear, and listened silently to what he said to them with big smiles on their faces. They still seemed to expect him to come climbing out of the phone. They thought the whole thing was magic.

If she called John from here so that he didn't

get the machine at her place, he'd want to know where she was—not in a demanding way, but just because it was the kind of friendly question he often asked. Friendly or not, she hated the idea of explaining. She wasn't remotely ready to talk to John about Jake.

She had talked about him when they were first married. John knew about Anna, the breakup, the hurt and mess. At one point he'd been so mad he'd been ready to hunt Jake down. Stacey had expected an old-fashioned duel— gauntlets thrown to the ground, pistols at dawn, the works.

And I tried to defend him, she remembered. *I talked about how young we were, how we never could have made it work back then.*

I never really got Jake out of my system, did I? Not even when I was angry with him.

No wonder the marriage hadn't succeeded.

"I have to get the twins home," she blurted out, after a silence that had lasted too long.

"Do you have to be somewhere later?"

"Well, no, but I just…like to have them sleep in their own beds at night. They're outgrowing the portable crib, especially sharing it."

She described Ella's attempts to climb out of it, and out of her proper crib at home, not sure if she sounded as though she was making excuses. Then she heard her daughter's voice along the corridor. "Mo-mmm-eeee!"

Scrambling to get dressed. Just what she hadn't wanted.

Jake pulled on his jeans and sweater more quickly than she did. "Do you want me to go?"

"You'd better. I'll be there in a second."

He padded down the corridor in his bare feet while she fumbled with bra hook and tank top straps and boots, hearing Ella and Max both crying, now. When she entered the room, Jake had both twins held awkwardly in his arms. "I'm sorry. They don't know me well enough. I shouldn't have picked them up."

She held her hands out for them and he passed them across. She wouldn't be able to hold them both at once like this for much longer, they were getting so heavy! "Hey, you guys," she crooned. "This is a major overreaction, don't you think? Why so cranky? Jake, you don't have to stay in here for this."

He nodded, treating her words as a dismissal. Watching his tight, angular movements as he left the room, Stacey could read his complex reaction so easily. He looked as if he'd had a door slammed in his face.

Yes, Jake, you did, she said to him in her head, *but two-year-olds can't fake what they*

*feel. They don't feel comfortable with you yet,
and they're not going to pretend. It's best that
you left.*

She felt unhappy about pushing him away—
about making love with him and then reminding them both of all the ways he didn't fully
belong in her life.

Except that maybe he would be grateful for
this. After he'd recovered from the door-slam
feeling, he'd realize that he had no wish to
belong everywhere in her life, he only wanted
to belong in her bed.

The possibility rocked her, although it
shouldn't have come as a surprise. She already
had all the evidence she needed about what
kind of boundaries he had safely in place. She'd
chosen to ignore it. Incurable optimist or sucker
for punishment? That, she didn't know.

The twins settled after a few minutes. She
put them down, held their hands and said,
"Let's go downstairs."

She found Jake pacing the great room as he
spoke on the cordless phone. He had those
sleeves rolled again, showing his ropy
forearms, and he looked confident and in
control.

"Get her admitted," he said in a clipped
decisive way. "I would. I wouldn't mess around

on this, with her history." He listened for a moment. "No, don't apologize, Lindsay, you did the right thing to call. I'll see her Monday in the maternity unit, hopefully still pregnant." He listened again. "Yeah, you, too. Bye."

When he'd put the phone down, he saw Stacey and the twins and his face changed at once. The focused aura of professional confidence had gone and there was a smoky, unreadable look in its place. Wariness? "So..." he said slowly. "What did we decide about tonight?"

Vulnerability, she realized with a shock.

He felt vulnerable, the same way she did.

"I—I don't want to just say goodbye and go home, Jake, it's not that." She dropped her voice, because this next bit was even harder to say. "I'd love to spend the whole night with you."

"You would..."

"But could we make it at my place?"

His expression cleared. "Of course. Yes." He whooshed out an unconscious sigh of relief and suddenly they were both grinning at each other like happy, goofy idiots. He came toward her, laced his fingers together in the small of her back and whirled her around, then pulled her close and buried his face in her neck, where she felt the heat of his breath. "I'm so glad we got that sorted out."

"So am I."

"Now I'm trying to think what we can do."

"Oh…" she said vaguely. "Does it matter? Play around here for a bit, head to my place, get takeout for us for dinner, and Max and Ella can have eggs and fruit. That doesn't take up enough hours, does it?" Imagination deserted her and she spread her hands, helpless. "I don't care what we do."

"Neither do I. Pick up a DVD? Just talk and hang out and—"

"—act like we were fourteen. Perfect!"

"Stop grinning at me, Handley."

"Yeah, Logan? Why?"

"You're making my face ache."

"But in a good way, right?"

"Always," he said, and she knew she wanted the word to mean a lot more than it really did.

Chapter Seven

"Say, 'Bye-bye, Daddy,'" Stacey instructed Ella. She waited. So far, neither of the twins had ever said it, no matter how intently they appeared to listen to John saying it to them. "Go ahead, bye-bye, Daddy."

"Bye-bye, Daddy, uv you."

Omigosh! There! She did say it!

Stacey laughed and took the phone as Ella held it out. "Did you hear that, John?"

"Yes, but what was the second bit?"

"Uv you. I love you. It's what I always say to them when I drop them at day care. Bye-bye, sweetheart, I love you. Oh, wasn't it just darling?"

John laughed, too. "It was pretty neat, I have to admit. Can we get Max back for another try?"

"Uh, no, sorry, he's long gone, back to his new blocks."

"You bought them new blocks? I just bought them a set here at home, a big one. We should coordinate. And we shouldn't spoil them."

"We're not. These were a—a gift from a friend."

"Yeah?" What had he heard in her tone? "Valbona? Suzanne?" Her two closest friends, as he knew.

"No, not them. Listen, I should go. They're pretty tired, and—"

"I won't keep you."

There was a beat of silence between them, and she knew he was wondering about the friend she'd managed not to name—wondering if the friend was male, and, if so, what he meant in Stacey's life. Maybe there was no such thing as an amicable divorce. She knew John still hadn't forgiven himself for not winning her whole heart. And he hadn't forgiven *her* because she'd never given it to him.

He had a stubborn temperament, which could

be a good quality in a man when he also knew how to let go. John didn't, sometimes. He pushed too much. If he'd been a military commander in days gone by, he would still have been fighting long after his last man had fallen, with the enemy overrunning his doomed ground.

Heroic, but not useful.

She had a rush of remorse. They needed honesty if they were going to manage parenting and divorce. "Listen," she told him, "It's Jake, actually, who gave the blocks to the kids. Jake Logan."

"Jake *Logan?* The one who—?"

"Yes. Him. He's back in Portland. An ob-gyn specialist at the hospital."

"You should have told me."

"I am telling you."

"And you're seeing each other."

"I'm not sure if I'd define—"

"This is not a good idea, Stacey. Don't you remember what you said to me about what you went through with him before?" He didn't give her a chance to reply. "And there are Max and Ella to consider."

"I know all that…"

"I can't believe you would even contemplate—"

"…but at this stage there's nothing for us to discuss. You know I would never overlook Max and Ella's needs. I told you about the blocks because it felt wrong to hold it back, but please don't—"

"I will! I absolutely will say or do whatever I think is necessary! I'll tell you exactly what I think about it if there's any suggestion it's going to hurt the kids—"

"John…"

His voice dropped. "—or hurt you, Stacey! We don't hate each other, do we?"

"I hope not. I hope we never—"

"So I'm going to look out for you, even if you can't look out for yourself. Be careful. And take care of my kids!"

He hung up the phone before she could say anything more. They'd had too many of these conversations, a million prickly, unfinished sentences, cutting in on each other, seeing things differently, never getting it right no matter how hard they tried.

Because they had tried, in the beginning. They'd tried for years.

Her warm feeling after Ella's "Bye-bye Daddy, uv you," had totally disappeared.

And Jake must have overheard.

Some of it, anyway.

He stood in the doorway. "I should pack up the blocks, I'm thinking. The kids are getting a little wild again." He didn't mention John.

"I'll help."

The twins had already had their baths and were snug in pajamas and fluffy slippers. They'd eaten their soft-boiled eggs with toast soldiers dipped in, and their plates of cut-up fruit. They would be ready for sleep very soon, and Stacey was getting hungry. She and Jake had decided to order their takeout to eat once the house was peaceful.

They tidied the blocks together, involving the twins by turning it into a low-key game about colors. All the red blocks first, then all the blue, and the green and the yellow. It helped the twins to settle down, and they almost knew the colors now. "Lello," Max said. He found a couple of other colors that they'd missed under the couch. "Dween. Boo. More lello."

"They seem pretty bright," Jake commented.

"Not that you should sound so surprised about it, Logan. Their mother has a college degree."

"Their mother puts in a lot of effort. I didn't mean to sound surprised. Many kids don't learn to talk so well, and definitely don't learn things like colors so early, unless they hear it one-on-one."

"Well, thank you. I'm not hothousing them, or anything. But when I'm with them all day, it's natural to talk to them."

She was about to take the twins upstairs, but Jake's next words stopped her. "John didn't seem too happy about the blocks."

"You heard that."

"I'm sorry. I didn't intend to."

"It's okay. You should probably know. He's not… ready for me to start dating again." *Especially to start dating you, Jake Logan.*

"Is it his business?" Jake demanded. "Does he think he has those kinds of rights over you?"

"He thinks he has the right to make sure I don't mess up his kids."

"That's—!"

"No," she cut in quickly. "It's not feudal or dictatorial."

"No?"

"If I'm honest, I feel the same. If he included a date during his weekends with Max and Ella, I'd want to know something about her, something about the relationship and her attitudes. Is she going to think she can smack them and yell at them and shut them in their rooms if they do something they shouldn't? Is she going to want John to off-load them onto a sitter whenever she's around? Does she see herself as a potential stepmother, and if so, how does she feel about that? On the other hand, if she's only a casual fling, how would I feel about the twins discovering her in his bed in the morning, if there had been a different woman the time before? It's important, and you get protective. They're still so little…"

"And John is asking those same questions about me."

"He would be, yes. I'm sorry that's— You probably don't need the pressure of knowing that."

"I could have worked it out for myself, if I'd thought. You're right. It's natural." He frowned. "So you don't want me to stay till morning?"

"I want you to. But you'd better not."

"Okay. Are you giving me a curfew hour?"

"No, I'm not. Do I need to? Please don't turn it into—"

"Sorry. I'm sorry. I won't."

"I'd better, um…" she began awkwardly.

"Yes, take them upstairs. I'll order dinner. If I'm not here when you get back down, I've gone to pick it up." He rubbed his shoulder. "I'd like to get some air." They'd decided on Chinese food, and had already agreed on the dishes. They had similar wide-ranging tastes in food, enjoyed spice, liked to try new things.

Stacey hoped the tension over John's attitude wouldn't spoil anything.

"My mouth is watering already," she told Jake, hiding her doubts.

The steamy aromas of shrimp and soy sauce and spice filled Jake's car when he parked it in front of Stacey's garage. The house looked quiet from this angle, its painted wooden charm typical of the Lair Hill neighborhood, although muted in the darkness. Despite the apparent peacefulness, he steeled himself to find chaos and two crying children when he went to open the front door with the key she'd given him.

Turning it in the lock, he held his breath and listened.

Ah, quiet!

After completely exhausting two healthy adults with nothing more than typical toddler activity and behavior, Max and Ella must be safely in bed.

He brought the bag of hot food into the kitchen, where he found Stacey hunting up blue-and-white Chinese bowls, blue linen place mats, wineglasses and silverware. "Are we eating in front of the DVD?" he asked.

They'd decided on this earlier, and he'd somehow envisioned forking in the food direct from the cartons. He now realized how much this betrayed about his bachelor status. He ate this way at least three times a week.

"Yes," she answered, smiling, "but that doesn't mean we're not allowed to be elegant about it."

"I guess not." She probably knew exactly the way he usually ate. "I like your kitchen, by the way."

"Thank you. So do I."

The high-ceilinged space was crowded with interest and color, a far cry from his sleek, incomprehensible appliances in stainless steel. She still used an old-fashioned gas cooker that must date from the 1940s, and the rest of the room followed the same theme. Old wooden cabinets had been stripped and freshly stained, and the paintwork was done in warm cream with contrasting detail in porcelain blue.

On a high shelf sat a row of antique china teapots, and below them another row of more down-to-earth kitchen equipment—a set of heavy metal scales with cast-iron weights, a cast-iron mincer with a worn wooden handle, a couple of antique rolling pins, a Mixmaster that had to be one of the original models from the Fifties.

"Did someone—" dumb question, he realized

halfway through, but finished it anyway "—do this for you?"

"You mean a professional? A decorator?"

"It's all you, right?"

"Me and about twelve years of collecting. I love all these old appliances. The teapots, the rice and flour bins."

"Do you still use them?"

"Some are just for show, I admit. I wouldn't trust the power cord on the Mixmaster, even though the motor still runs just fine. I do have the modern necessities, as well, as you can see." She gestured to a blender on the countertop, and a dishwasher built in to the row of cabinets beneath it. "And I have about a hundred bone china teacups that used to sit on the bottom two shelves, here, but they're packed away until the twins get more civilized and I have more time to dust. Shall we take all this to the coffee table? Don't want to be eating cold shrimp."

"Could we eat here, instead? Talk a bit, have some wine and save the DVD for later?" Jake heard himself say.

Considering he'd recently accused Stacey of being stuck in a suburban rut, he was surprisingly curious about everything she had to say. And considering he used to enjoy shoveling takeout into his mouth too fast with no one around to remind him about table manners, he now discovered that the idea of avoiding his recent bouts of heartburn by eating slowly while he and Stacey talked held an unexpected appeal.

"Sure," she said.

"Eating on our own in front of TV is…"

"…probably something both of us do too often."

"You, too, huh?"

"Since the divorce."

"I eat too fast."

"Me, too." She made a fist and a sour face, and tapped her chest. "Which do you go for? The liquid or the pills?"

"I don't think either of 'em work real well. I usually just sit up too late cursing chili."

They both laughed, and laid her elegant place settings on the kitchen table instead.

It was such a good evening. With his palate spoiled by authentic oriental cuisine eaten in places like Hong Kong, Sydney and New York's Chinatown, Jake discovered Stacey knew how to find a good Chinese restaurant even in suburban Portland. The wine slipped down easily, a glass and a half each, sipped slowly over a good hour or more of talk.

At around nine, they loaded the dishwasher,

stacked the cartons of leftover food in the fridge and made themselves comfortable on her squishy couch to watch their movie, which had enough laughs mixed in with its romance to lull him into thinking that chick flicks, as his brother Scott called them, weren't so bad after all. Jake put his arm around Stacey's shoulder and she nestled into him and they stayed that way until the end credits rolled.

Then he made some token murmurs about getting home and she told him not to be an idiot and they went upstairs to bed.

They made love more slowly this time. More thoughtfully. More experimentally. A little more conversation in the mix. She kissed and touched every inch of him, turning it into the most erotic and sensual massage he'd ever imagined. He grew painfully aroused and at the same time as relaxed as a lion sleeping in the sun. She felt like a big cat, too—so sinuous and sleek and soft. When he entered her at last, they barely needed to move. Their bodies were so sensitized and attuned, so ready.

So ready.

And then so sleepy.

He barely stayed awake long enough to hear her drowsy murmur of his name. "Sorry," she finished. "Too sleepy to tell you. Amazing."

"Don't have to say it," he answered. "I know."

The clock beside her bed read 3:12 when he awoke—suddenly, the way he did when his hospital pager sounded, or when he was in a hotel room and at the mercy of a new city's unfamiliar sounds. One of the twins must be having a vivid dream. He heard a little cry and some fragments of unhappy words coming from along the corridor. He lay there, muscles tensed, wondering what to do.

Should he go to their room?

Remembering Max and Ella's reaction to him when they'd awoken from their naps this afternoon, he decided against it. If the words turned into crying, Stacey would wake up and do whatever she usually did, and that would be best.

Forcing himself to relax, he listened for more sounds but none came, and the sweet, sleeping female body lying warm beside him didn't stir. He felt her slow, rhythmic breathing nudge his side, in and out, in and out.

Rhythm.

Rhythm was nice.

Maybe he hadn't had enough of it in recent years. The rhythm of someone else's breathing, because he'd too often slept alone. The rhythm of the seasons, because travel had dislocated them and turned them upside down—scorching hot Christmas in Australia, steamy humidity any month of the year in Cambodia where he'd done three short-term stints as a medical volunteer.

After the last of those, he'd flown direct to Denver where the landscape had been covered in February snow. Even the rhythm of a day-to-day routine wasn't familiar, because obstetricians kept odd hours and single obstetricians kept the oddest hours of all with no family to anchor them.

Yes, the rhythms of an ordinary life had a definite appeal.

He felt in no hurry to get back to sleep, slipped his arm around Stacey and buried his nose in her shampoo-scented hair. He would sleep again eventually, and then morning would come, heralded no doubt by a pair of alarm clocks disguised as children. Stacey said she went to them pretty fast now, as soon as she heard them, because they eagerly attempted to climb out of their big cribs as well as the little portable one she'd brought to his place, and she thought their climbing efforts would soon succeed.

Morning.

Max and Ella finding him in their mother's bed.

Stacey didn't want it to happen, he remembered.

She'd talked about it in relation to John and a potential new girlfriend. She'd sounded emotional about it, and she'd made sense.

"If he had a casual fling, how would I feel about the twins discovering a woman in his bed in the morning? It's important, and you get protective," she'd said.

Oh, but he couldn't leave. How the hell could he leave? The bed felt so warm, and Stacey felt so good beside him. He could imagine them both awaking at the first hint of dawn, warmth turning to heat, making love again…

And the twins picking today to learn the crib climb and showing up in Mommy's bedroom all proud of their new achievement, right in the middle of the action.

Pond scum.

I must be, Jake thought, *because I'd take the risk. We'd stop if we heard them. We'd have the covers pulled up.*

He had a whole raft of easy rationalizations on the subject.

Because he really didn't want to leave.

Stacey stirred in her sleep and unconsciously snuggled closer. Jake couldn't see clearly in the darkness, but he could swear she had a smile on her face. If he slept through until morning, what was she going to do about it? Would it be such a terrible crime?

She stirred a little more and he thought that if she woke up, then he'd ask.

He waited, hoping, wondering if he could, say, tap her shoulder or tickle her. But then she half rolled in the bed and he heard her breathing deepen and slow once more. He knew he had to go, as she'd asked.

Quietly, he slid to the edge of the bed, flipped back the corner of the comforter and climbed out. Gathering his clothes, he took them into the bathroom and dressed there. He kept listening for any sound coming from the bedroom, but all stayed silent.

Downstairs, he found pen and scrap paper in the kitchen and wrote out a note.

"As per our earlier discussion, I'm going home." He hesitated. The statement sounded too stilted and formal, and yet he didn't want to write it in words of one syllable.

You told me you didn't want the twins to find me in your bed.

That sounded… accusatory, somehow, as if he was telling her, "You're being a pain, but I'm going along with it."

After some more thought, he decided that there was an appropriate jauntiness to what he'd written. It didn't come across as too heavy, and that was good. He added, "I'll call you. You're fabulous. Jake."

He drove home in the dark. There was a fine slush on the roads, making them slippery. His bed felt cold and too new. Two hours later his pager sounded and it was Dr. Lindsay Forrest again, to let him know that Mrs. Murchison's symptoms hadn't settled down, in fact they'd gotten worse, and it seemed unavoidable that they'd have to deliver.

Did Jake want to do it? Mrs. Murchison was asking for him, and Lindsay herself was a little nervous about the whole case. The triplets were at twenty-six weeks' gestation. They would be dangerously premature, all three of them were badly positioned in the womb and one triplet's placenta lay far too low.

He dressed again and drove to the hospital.

Stacey found Jake's note as soon as she went downstairs with the twins at six-thirty.

Well, she was looking for a note, so it wasn't hard to see.

"As per our earlier discussion," it began.

Still creaky from sleep and not even dressed, while the twins acted as if they were ready to run a marathon, she couldn't think. What earlier discussion? Finally, while the coffee dripped through the filter and Max and Ella ate cereal, she thought she'd worked it out. He meant the discussion about him staying the whole night.

She read the note again. "As per our earlier discussion, I'm going home." It sounded prickly, in her head, as if she'd put his nose out of joint with her overprotective insistence. She couldn't remember the "discussion" word for word. She knew it hadn't lasted long, a couple of quick lines when she was heading upstairs to put the twins to bed.

"I'll call you. You're fabulous," sounded a lot better than the first part, but still she wasn't sure.

He'd call her when?

He'd gone home when?

And she was fabulous where? Just in bed? Or maybe in a couple of other significant rooms, as well? Such as the kitchen, where they'd had that great conversation while they ate?

This was the kind of thing women always obsessed over when they shouldn't. An hour of going over the whole evening—in fact the whole of yesterday—didn't leave her with any more insight or certainty regarding Jake, his note or his feelings than she'd had after the first five minutes.

She'd known from the start that she was laying

her whole heart on the line by getting involved with him again. She'd gone into it with her eyes open and her courage high. But the courage had ebbed a little, and the obsessing didn't help.

"Don't you sometimes wish you had a Y chromosome, honey?" she said to her daughter. "Sooo convenient on the potty, and in the area of relationship analysis, too. And isn't it great that you don't understand most of the words in what I just said?"

Ella agreed. "Go outside?" she asked hopefully, in reply. Max thought this was such a great idea, he ran at once to get his shoes.

"How about we wait on it a little, my sweethearts?" Stacey suggested. "Like until the sun actually comes up?"

She somehow thought she couldn't expect Jake to call, either, until the sun had properly risen in the sky. Men were completely unreasonable about things like that.

Women could be pretty unreasonable, also. Stacey listened to her messages from yesterday, and along with a couple of telemarketer hangups, there was another one from her sister. "Hi-ee! Just calling to chat. Did you get my message last week? Call if you get this. Love you and miss you! Bye-ee!"

Stacey called Giselle back at nine, when the

sun had well and truly risen behind the low clouds and Jake would have to know that a mother of toddler twins was up, dressed, breakfasted and more than ready for some phone action.

The theory was that Stacey calling Giselle would make Jake call Stacey—this was the unreasonable part—and the call waiting tone would break into her conversation with Giselle and she'd be able to tell him in an offhand manner, "I'm already on another call, so can I get back to you?" as if she hadn't been hanging out to hear his voice for two hours.

"I'm sorry I didn't call you back," she told her sister.

"No sweat," Giselle trilled. "I didn't even think about it until yesterday. I have been sooo busy! You wouldn't believe it!" She listed several glittering social engagements, and the outfits she'd had to purchase for each. "Stirling is climbing the ladder of success so fast he's burning his hands on the rungs. He's just having a dream run." She detailed various proofs of her husband's success, including the fact that some celebrity executive wife was being sooo friendly, "practically treats me like a baby sister, the things she confides in me."

"That's great, Giselle."

What wasn't so great was the ominous

silence she could hear from the living room, where the twins were playing. Hurrying in there with the cordless phone still pressed to her ear, she found that Max and Ella had somehow taken an opened packet of breadcrumbs from the pantry and were now totally absorbed in spreading the crumbs in a very exciting layer of smooth crumbiness all over the seat of the couch with the splayed palms of their little hands.

Suppressing her stricken cry, Stacey accepted that the mess would have to wait until Giselle had finished her gushing account of life's recent successes. Twenty minutes later, after her sister had failed to ask a single question about the twins or Stacey herself, she put down the phone, wondering if she only existed in Giselle's world as an envious listening ear, and if even calling their relationship *amicable* was a stretch.

No call waiting tone from Jake had interrupted the conversation.

Almost noon, Jake saw as he poured himself a tired cup of coffee in the on-call room.

Almost noon, with three triplets surviving and now in the hands of specialist pediatricians and nurses, while their mother had lost a scary amount of blood during her dramatic post-partum hemorrhage but had survived, too.

He felt wiped.

His blue scrub suit showed the evidence of his expert work, and his head wouldn't slow down. Those tiny babies were not out of the woods, yet. Even though their care and survival fell outside of his professional boundaries, he kept thinking about their odds and his role.

Mrs. Murchison had wanted to breast-feed as a supplement to formula, but she might not have the strength to establish an adequate milk supply. The babies would need tube feeding at this point. They were all on ventilators. They'd been conceived through IVF and they'd be the only children Kathy Murchison would have after what he'd had to do to bring her bleeding under control.

He could make it home now, for a few hours, but he wanted to come back and check on her again later in the day. Lindsay Forrest, the junior obstetrician who'd been covering for him this weekend, had performed well during the crisis. She could probably have gotten through it safely without his presence, but he was glad she'd called him in, all the same.

The time he'd spent with Stacey last night seemed like days ago rather than hours.

Reaching home, he changed into casual clothes and tossed his soiled surgical scrubs in the laundry hamper, glad that he had house-keeping help starting part-time tomorrow. He found a red plastic block behind the kitchen door and wondered how it had gotten there. Clutched in a toddler hand and then dropped at random, probably.

His otherwise immaculate residence showed further signs of little hands. There was a smear of yesterday's lunch on the mirrorlike front surface of the dishwasher, a wet leaf in the mudroom sink and a squished berry remnant on the floor.

Why, when he was so tired and getting very hungry, was he touring every room like this, searching for signs of Max and Ella's mess?

Because of his mixed feelings about their mother.

Because he was pond scum.

"I'll call you," he'd written to Stacey in his note.

But when?

Now?

He thought about it, felt the tension in his muscles, the frustration still simmering inside him at the reality of triplets born fourteen weeks early via a difficult Cesarean delivery. He didn't want to call Stacey now, didn't trust his negative mood to stay safely out of the way. He would end up trampling on the whole conversation with some ill-thought comment. He knew he would.

In fact, he should hold off on calling her for a couple of days, until he'd had a chance to think, and get some perspective. For both their sakes, he had to be careful not to get too close. They'd had a fantastic night, tuned to each other in bed like instruments in an orchestra, but that wasn't the point. It was only a fraction of what really mattered.

To get some distance, he went out, grabbed a drive-through burger for lunch and hit a couple of cycling stores in search of the perfect bike to use in one of the country's most bicycle-friendly cities. Keen to get his fitness up to its peak again after finding too little time for exercise in recent weeks, he came away with a top-of-the-range machine that left him several thousand dollars poorer.

In passing, he noted that there were more options for carrying or towing small children on a bicycle than he'd ever realized before.

Chapter Eight

"Kids, you want pita?" Stacey's friend Valbona called down her basement stairs. "Is out of oven five minutes."

Stacey stretched reluctantly in the comfortable armchair and picked up her empty mug, ready to return it to the kitchen. "We should go, Valbona." It was almost five o'clock on a Wednesday afternoon. There would be traffic. She still had to stop at the store, and she was working tomorrow and Friday, as usual. She had to make some attempt to get her house in order and meals planned for the next two days.

"Nooo!" Valbona protested. "Stay for pita. Kids love it."

The kids did. So did Stacey. "Ten more minutes," she conceded.

"You take with you, too."

"Really? You have enough?"

Valbona dismissed the question with an impatient gesture and poured them both another cup of coffee. "I need to finish other dough," she said.

"May I help?"

"Of course."

"You're nice, because you know I'm going to ruin it."

"Is okay. Dough is good, you can't ruin it. Only when *you* make dough, then is ruined."

"Yeah, the one time I tried! I'll wait until you get to the easy part."

Stacey stood back and sipped her coffee, watching Valbona at work. The dough she had made was incredibly soft and elastic, and she stretched it in a paper-thin and almost translucent layer until it covered the entire rectangular surface of the table, which was covered in a plastic-lined cloth.

Valbona had learned the technique from her mother as a child in the isolated valley where she was born. Then, it had been part of Yugoslavia. Now it was a neglected and unsafe part of Serbia, which Valbona Demiri and her husband and three children had been forced to flee in 1999 and had come to the U.S.A. as refugees.

They'd met when Stacey and John had owned a house with a small mother-and-daughter apartment attached, and had rented it out to the Demiri family. The friendship was an unlikely one, on the surface. It managed to cross the communication barrier of Valbona's fractured English, and to ignore their vastly different backgrounds. Shared values and shared humor were the things that made it work.

"You want to do spinach and cheese?" Valbona asked.

"Yes, and then see if I can roll the whole thing up the way you do."

Stacey took the bowl of freshly chopped spinach, yogurt and feta cheese that Valbona handed her and spooned it in a scattered pattern over the stretched-out dough. Then she lifted up one side of the tablecloth while Valbona lifted the other, and the sheet of dough miraculously rolled itself down the sloping cloth on each side to end up in a twin sausage shape right across the middle. "There! I didn't mess it up!"

"Nice!" Valbona rolled the sausage into a spiral, set it in a circular baking pan brushed with melted butter, and put it in the oven. "Other one is ready," she said. She took it out and cut it into rough squares then set them on a platter. "Is too hot for now."

"Yes, I won't call them, yet."

The twins were playing in the basement of the Demiri's small house with their middle daughter Zaida, who was almost thirteen and itching to be allowed to babysit. Valbona and her husband were conservative on this subject. Not until she was fourteen, they had decreed, and then only for people like Stacey, whom they knew well. Stacey understood their protective instincts, and knew she'd probably share them when Max and Ella reached their teen years—a point which still seemed unimaginably far in the future, although Valbona had promised her, "Is like next week."

Next week? When it was more than ten years away? And when *this* week had seemed like half a year, because Jake still hadn't called?

Valbona handed Stacey a piece of hot pita on a plate and she bit into it without her usual appetite for the springy pastry and salty flavors. Should she tell Valbona how she was feeling? Her heart sank at the idea. It seemed too hard.

Sali Demiri's courtship of his wife had lasted the traditional length of time in their culture— roughly thirty seconds, from what Stacey could work out. He had come to her family's house with some mutual friends who had told him— truthfully—that Valbona was very beautiful and an excellent housekeeper. The men had sat in the living area, and Valbona had come out from the kitchen bearing a platter of cakes she had made. She'd laid them on the table and returned to the kitchen, where the women sat. Sali's friends had turned to him and asked, "Well?" while Valbona was similarly questioned in the kitchen.

They'd both said yes.

The next time they'd met was at their wedding.

They'd now been married for eighteen years, and though they sometimes yelled at each other—you could pick up on yelling, even when it was in Albanian—Stacey knew they were happy.

All of which added up to her feeling that she couldn't possibly be pathetic and spineless enough to wail to her friend, "Why-y hasn't he ca-alled?"

After another sip of coffee and a mouthful of pita, she did it anyhow. Valbona listened and nodded. "He want to see how much you are upset, so he know how much you like him."

Stacey shook her head. "I don't think he works that way."

"You like him?"

"Yes."

"And he like you?"

"I—I'm pretty sure."

Valbona shrugged. "So he is busy, and soon he call."

There.

Simple.

Stacey hugged her friend. "You're good for me, Valbona."

Valbona shrugged again, and grinned. "Is no expensive."

Stacey arrived home with the twins an hour later, after Max and Ella had been a little too "helpful" in the supermarket, to find the phone ringing. Picking up, she heard John's familiar greeting.

"I'm in town overnight for a meeting," he said. "Can I drop over and see you and the twins, since I can't take them this weekend?"

"Of course you can. If you'd let me know, I could have planned something more interesting for dinner."

"I was hoping to get home tonight, but we didn't finish so we're having another session tomorrow. I couldn't have let you know any sooner. Don't worry about dinner. I'll eat whatever comes."

"Soup and toasted cheese sandwiches?"

"Is fine."

Despite each eating a piece of pita at Valbona's, Max and Ella were both hungry. Stacey quickly took out a container of frozen homemade soup and thawed it in the microwave. While it circled around, she cut slices of cheese and tomato and buttered bread. John arrived just as she'd transferred the beef-and-vegetable soup into a pot on the stove to heat through.

He gave her a quick hug, looking a little stressed. He'd had his dark hair cut since she'd last seen him and the style was too severe and close-cropped for the shape of his head. Hair grew, she reminded herself. But it was no good. These little things about him always grated on her more than they should.

"Mmm, smells good in here," he said. "Where are the guys?"

"In front of the electronic babysitter, because they're pooped. They've had a busy day. Just ask the shelf packers at the mini-mart."

John winced. "You didn't strap them in the shopping cart?"

"The store was busy. There were no carts."

She added, "I tried bribing this woman fifty dollars to hand hers over, but she wouldn't. We practically had a sword fight with our bread sticks right there in the baked goods aisle."

"Huh? Stacey! You shouldn't do things like that! And fifty dollars? Don't you think that's—?"

"Joking, John."

He looked chastened. "Sorry. Ha ha. Of course you were. I'm still thinking about that meeting."

He did have a sense of humor, she knew. He just forgot to put it into gear sometimes. She watched him as he left the kitchen and went in search of the twins. Their whole marriage had been like this—like an alluring photo printed with the colors crooked, or a piano played fluently but badly out of tune. So close to being right, and yet so jarringly, hopelessly wrong.

The doorbell rang.

Still thinking about what had gone wrong between herself and John, she went to answer it, expecting a kid selling cookies for a sports team trip, or some other typical dinner-hour interruption.

Instead, Jake stood there, wearing hospital scrubs with a sweater and a leather jacket on top. Weirdly, it worked. "Hi. I said I'd call, but then I—" he shrugged "—came by, instead."

Thinking that next time she went into a relationship she would be sorely tempted to try Valbona and Sali's bring-in-a-plate-of-cookies-and-say-yes-after-thirty-seconds approach, Stacey manufactured a bright smile. "Great! Come in and meet John!"

So this was John.

Instantly, Jake didn't like him. The man was...

He studied the twins' father covertly, looking for reasons to justify his unease. Dark hair, neat suit, gray eyes, competent build. Ella had a fistful of his trousers held tight in her hand, crumpling the fabric, and John didn't seem to mind.

Okay, at first impression there was nothing outwardly wrong with him, but still there was somehow an underlying sense that he was...

Stacey's ex-husband.

Face it, Jake. That's the only reason you don't like him. You're looking for logic and justification, but there isn't any. This is as primitive as two stags clashing antlers over the right to dominate the herd. "Olympia's a nice little city," he said to the man, taking bland small talk to new depths.

Sports would have been a better choice.

How 'bout those Huskies?

"I like the job," John replied. "But it's one of those political things that doesn't recognize the existence of weekends. I really haven't gotten to know the city." The tone was cool and distant, the glance flinty and skeptical.

John didn't like him, either, Jake could tell.

In fact John really, *really* didn't like him.

If Stacey and I keep seeing each other, I'll have to deal with this, he realized. Deal with my feelings, and his, because he's not going away. He's the father of these kids, and I haven't worked out how I'm going to deal with them, yet, either. I've stayed away from her for forty-eight hours longer than I wanted to, and nothing is any clearer.

His temples tightened, suddenly, and his stomach soured.

Hell, he shouldn't have come. He wouldn't have, if he'd had any idea that John might be here.

His fault. If he'd called Stacey as he'd told her he would, it wouldn't have happened.

"Dinner's almost on the table," she chirped. Jake could see how tense she was. She turned to him and asked brightly, "Will you stay? There's plenty."

"Uh, no, I'm on call tonight, and I have a patient in labor. I may have to head back at any moment." Which he wouldn't have let get in the way if Stacy and the twins had been alone.

Both of them knew it. Their eyes met, and there was a flash of complicated understanding. "Well, I might see you at the hospital tomorrow, then."

"Yes." He planned to make sure of it, but wasn't prepared to say so in front of John.

"How about a quick drink before you go?" John suggested, taking both Jake and Stacey by surprise.

"I don't drink when I'm on call."

"Doesn't have to be alcohol. Stacey?"

"I have juice or soda water, coffee, obviously," she listed obediently. "Milk…"

He wants more of a chance to check me out, Jake understood. He said aloud, "I'll take a juice."

Because two could play that game.

Stacey said they could hold dinner for a little if she gave the twins their soup. She switched on the gas fire, poured the drinks and Jake and John sat in front of it while she attempted to do the same in between checking on the progress of the soup into Max and Ella's mouths in the kitchen. Jake realized he should have suggested that they all sit in that cozy kitchen, and immediately—with a spurt of satisfaction—labeled John inconsiderate because he hadn't done so.

Aha! He's inconsiderate! That's why they're divorced!

Logan, you are not only pond slime, you are pathetic *pond slime.*

He decided to try harder. What was it that Dad had said about forgiveness in his second book? Act as if you've forgiven someone, even when you haven't. If you act it well enough, then genuine forgiveness will eventually catch up. Dad had expressed it more fluently—Jake was no writer—but the basic argument was there.

He would act as if he liked John, and one day maybe he really would.

If he was still in Portland.

If he was still seeing Stacey.

If he wasn't, then he'd never have to think about John Deroy again and none of this emotional complexity would matter.

The sense of instant freedom that came with this idea fought a bitter battle inside him with an even more powerful anticipation of loss. Leaving Stacey's house a half hour later, he couldn't label the visit a success.

"Stacey, do you have a minute?" Jillian Logan stood in the doorway of Stacey's office in the main hospital building.

"Could you make do with forty-five seconds?" She'd had a busy day so far, and if she didn't get a lunch break soon, the offerings still available at the staff cafeteria would not appeal.

"Uh, well, since my *minute* was actually a euphemism for *half an hour if we're lucky…*" Jillian made an apologetic face.

"What's the problem?"

"There were some files over at Children's Connection that we never got straightened out after the problems three years ago."

"And *we never got straightened out* is a euphemism for *are still lost,* right?"

"You never met Charlie Prescott. He was a piece of work. I suspect he destroyed as much as he could. Fortunately, we've replaced most of the lost information with duplicates from various files here at the hospital, but there's a particular adoption… I don't want to go into too many details in writing for reasons of patient confidentiality, so I didn't want to e-mail you about this. There's a particular memo I'm looking for, which may be some-where in the system. I'll write down a couple of names which may help. If you have time."

"That's the only detail you can give?"

"You've met a couple of the people involved. One of them is Lisa Sanders. The birth father of her baby is threatening to reenter the picture and challenge the validity of the adoption. She and the adoptive parents—Brian and Carrie—they were at the potluck, too—are very concerned, and so am I. Lisa is the last person in the world who deserves something like this, and Brian and Carrie don't, either. If the threat comes to anything, it's going to tear them apart."

She gave Stacey some more information and then hurried away to her next appointment, but although Stacey tried every search strategy she could think of and spent more time on the problem than she could afford, she couldn't find the relevant memo. She had just decided to abandon the search, giving a couple of final aggressive clicks to her mouse as she closed some files, when there came a light tap at her open office door and Jake entered.

"What's up?" he said at once. He must have heard the frustrated sound she'd made. In dark trousers and a lightly patterned shirt and tie, he looked gorgeous, competent, authoritative, familiar... Her whole world shifted at the sight of him.

"Nothing." She stood up, foolishly flustered by his unexpected appearance, after last night, when John's presence had made everything so awkward. She didn't want to mention Lisa Sanders's problem, despite the association with the Logan family and Children's Connection. "I have issues with the hospital computer system."

"I think you can get counseling for that now."

Her stomach rumbled, and she murmured wryly, "Lunch would probably do."

"You want me to ask you to lunch?"

"No, no." Is that what he thought? That she was hinting at an invitation? "I just meant it's after one-thirty, I spent longer on this computer search than I meant to and I'm hungry. It's not your problem."

"Relax, Stacey." His voice dropped. "That's actually why I came by. To take you to lunch, if you were free. We didn't get a chance to talk last night." He leaned a hand against the doorway, standing a little too close to be appropriate if anyone walked by. Stacey didn't care—she wanted him closer.

"No. I was disappointed about that, too," she said.

Saturday already seemed too long ago.

Too many heartbeats. Too many complications. Too much time to think.

Stacey knew herself. She never took any relationship lightly. She was so determined to remain on good terms with John, for example, and was way more disappointed in her shallow connection with her sister than she liked to admit, even to herself. She'd only slept with Jake because she hoped for more, and if they ended up with nothing, the wounds would take a long time to heal. Going into the whole thing with her eyes open didn't give her the power she needed to shield her heart.

"John seems like a decent guy," Jake said smoothly. "I liked him."

"No, you didn't! Neither of you could stand each other," she blurted out, then clapped her mouth shut and closed her eyes, horrified.

She opened them again almost at once, when Jake laughed softly, brushed his hand along her jaw and tapped the door shut with one Italian-loafer-clad foot. "Okay, you got me," he said. "Guilty as charged."

"I shouldn't have said it."

"I'm glad you did. There's no point in lying. I *tried* to like him, okay? I wanted to like him."

"I don't think he wants to like you."

"No. Well. That's another issue. Something to work on."

"You're prepared to do that? To work on liking John?"

Was that a beat of hesitation?

"Let's not talk about this now," he said. "Let's go to lunch. How much time do you have?"

"Oh, say, forty-five minutes, minus the forty-two minutes I spent digging around in the stupid computer."

"Three minutes. Same here, my next appointment is at two. So we're good to go."

She laughed and let go of all the negative, circular thoughts that had gone around and around in her head since Sunday. He was here beside her, in the same space, breathing the same air, smiling at her and clearly looking forward to lunch, and for the moment this was all that mattered.

At the cafeteria, she chose a salad and some juice, while Jake ordered a Mexican wrap and they found a relatively quiet corner table. He told her about his new bicycle, waxing poetic about the precision engineering. "It satisfies me when something really works, when it's been made with so much attention to the right detail. I know it's only a bicycle, but…"

"No, I know what you mean. I'm guessing that you didn't buy the bargain model."

"Uh, no."

"I guess those things can run into hundreds of dollars." She knew Portland was considered an excellent place for cycling, but had never done any as an adult herself. She'd outgrown her last bicycle at the age of ten.

"Again, no," Jake said. "Try thousands."

"Thousands? Wow! You have to show me this bicycle!"

"I will if you promise to wash your hands before you touch it."

"There must be more to this sport than I'd realized."

"There is. I haven't done any cycling since I was in Australia, and I'm looking forward to getting back to it. Come to dinner tonight and you can see my new toy then." Again, she thought she detected the smallest hesitation before he added, "Bring the twins. Don't get a sitter."

"Are you sure you want the twins coming anywhere near your bicycle?"

"We might leave the bicycle display until they're…" He stopped, then continued, "I was going to say until they're asleep, but maybe that doesn't work. You wouldn't want to have to bring their portable crib and then wake them up to go home. And I know the issue of staying over is awkward, too."

"I'll get a sitter, if I can."

He said cautiously, "Maybe that's best."

Stacey felt a little eddy of apprehension. She and Jake had slipped so easily into their old familiarity with each other, but it was an illusion in many ways. Seventeen years had gone by. They were different people now. She was a parent, with a divorce under her belt, and there were only a handful of life events that could change a person as much as motherhood and a failed marriage. She had to remember how new and untested this all was, and how many pitfalls could lie ahead.

Suddenly, she didn't know if seeing Jake was a courageous act on her part, or the most foolish thing she'd ever done.

Chapter Nine

Stacey got a sitter.

But when she called Jake to tell him so, she sounded a little prickly and stilted, and he said quickly, "I'm sorry, would this whole idea have worked better if we'd made it your place, instead? Do you want to change the plan?"

"It's fine. I'm leaving to pick her up in five minutes."

"That soon?" he asked, without thinking, as if he was calling into question the efficiency of her arrangements.

His heart sank when she felt compelled to explain, "She's not my regular girl, but a friend of hers. She's great, but she lives farther away and has no transport. By the time I load the kids in the car, drive to her place, get back here, get the twins settled with her, get out to you... You told me seven, right?"

"I'm sorry. Make it later if you want."

"It's fine. Don't expect me on the dot, though. Unexpected things happen."

"You must only have gotten home about half an hour ago."

"Twenty minutes. But everything's under control. More or less." Sudden crying in the background punctuated her statement.

Jake cursed his own thoughtlessness and didn't know if a third apology would help. He'd envisaged a simple, easy evening. No dressing up, no frantic schedule, no pressure. They'd both worked all day. Instead, he'd apparently imposed a complicated timetable on Stacey, with all sorts of unnecessary driving and disruption to the twins' routine.

How could he have gotten so far out of his depth? He felt as if twelve years of college-level education, financial security, world travel and success in a demanding profession had left him less equipped to handle the complexities of Stacey's existence than he had been seventeen years ago.

He offered, "Would it help if I picked the sitter up?"

"Jake, I deal with these kinds of arrangements all the time. It's in place. Let's leave it. Just…you know…give me something to eat that's not kid food, okay?"

He laughed, "I'll refreeze the fish fingers, then, and ditch the mac-and-cheese."

She arrived at twenty after seven, with her hair freshly brushed and lip gloss glistening on her mouth. She wore a soft kind of top with a V-neck in a pattern of warm swirly floral colors, and figure-hugging black trousers with a smear of mint-green toothpaste on the butt.

She obviously didn't know about the toothpaste, and Jake decided not to tell her.

He'd already made enough mistakes for one evening.

Hopefully the food wouldn't be one of them, however. If the catering firm didn't show with the four gourmet courses he'd ordered over the phone, then it was really true that money couldn't buy everything because they were expensive!

Worth it.

Worth every cent.

They sat in his sleek, never-used dining room at Stacey's request and lingered over lobster ravioli, goat cheese salad, steak with pepper sauce and grilled vegetables and chocolate truffle cake. She pointed her fork at him during dessert and spoke with a thick, shiny bead of chocolate on her lower lip. "I cannot tell you how much better this is than mac-and-cheese!"

He wanted to lick the bead of chocolate away, and wondered if they could skip coffee and go straight to sex instead. After a covert glance at his watch a few seconds later, he wondered if they'd have time to get to sex at all. It was already well after nine, and when he considered the logistics of her return journey, and dropping the sitter home...

"Will you leave the kids on their own while you run the sitter back to her place?" he blurted out, and watched her face drop in horror.

"On their *own?* I'll put her in a cab!"

"Right. Of course."

"On their own, Jake?"

"I thought... They're asleep, you wouldn't want to wake them up."

"It gives me chills even thinking about it." She shook her head.

"I wasn't thinking. Of course you couldn't leave them alone. But that must mean even a trip to the store for milk..."

"...becomes a military exercise, and not

something that can be attempted after bath-
time," she finished for him, with exaggerated
patience. "Welcome to the world of the single
parent."

He wished they'd never trespassed onto the
subject. It forced him to think about all the
issues he hadn't yet seriously addressed. What
was it they'd said to each other last Tuesday
night? That their relationship had gone up a
couple of notches from amicable? He knew
what had to come next—what had to come
soon if they were going to keep seeing each
other. He had to decide how much he was
prepared to give, and what compromises he
was prepared to make.

And he had to find out how much Stacey
would consider enough, and whether she
would walk away if he couldn't give it all.

Not tonight, his body said. She hadn't yet
licked that bead of chocolate from her lip, and
his glance kept arrowing toward it while he remembered the feel of her mouth, the taste of
her, the sounds she made when they kissed. He
wasn't going to get sidetracked by a difficult
emotional confrontation tonight.

*Admit it, Logan—you're still pond scum, and
you're still scared.*

A helpless prisoner of his own need, he half

stood in his chair and leaned across the table toward her. "Something is driving me nuts right now," he muttered. "You have chocolate on your lower lip."

"Oh." She began to lift her finger and her lips parted. He saw the tip of her tongue, but before she could lick her lower lip, his mouth closed over hers with the chocolate still in place and he tasted it, tasted the sweetness of the sugar and cocoa butter and cream in both their mouths and never wanted the kiss to end.

"I have a confession, Logan, I just can't handle threesomes," Stacey murmured against Jake's mouth. "This table is getting in the way."

"How about with it under us, instead of between us?"

She laughed. "Then it would be a tensome, with all those dirty dishes."

He let her go. The breaking of contact almost hurt, she wanted him back so much. He came around to her and pulled the tablecloth to one side on the way, taking the dishes with it. "There. Enough space now?"

He couldn't be planning to lift her onto the—

He was. He splayed his hands around her upper thighs, and with one efficient crunch of his stomach muscles he'd hoisted her onto the slippery smooth surface of the polished rosewood. "Jake…"

"Wrap your legs around me." She wrapped her arms around his neck, instead. "I said legs," he growled.

"Jake…"

"You want this."

So help her, she did, and she possessed as little patience as he had. She felt herself start to shake. The trembling was like an adrenaline rush after a scare, or a sugar hit after a morning on the run with no time to eat. The need was so physical, the hunger so great.

She buried her face in the fabric of his shirt and inhaled his smell like an addictive drug. The dense strength of his body captivated her hands. She ran them across his back, exploring him, claiming him, learning every nuance of his shape off by heart.

He ran his hands down her inner thighs, parting them so that she could do as he'd asked and imprison him with her legs. His touch was intimate and sure. Then he pressed his body forward and she felt the hard nudge of his arousal. "Our clothes," she gasped.

"We'll get to that at our own good speed."

She loved what he promised with the words—that there was time to experience this to the full. She kissed him again, pressing her cheek to his, then turning her face, sliding her mouth across his warm skin, finding moisture and readiness. She'd never known such arousing, sensual kisses. He engulfed her mouth, couldn't get deep enough, mimicking with his tongue the more intimate thrusting they both craved.

When he finally tried to peel her top up over her head, he moved a little clumsily, but that was good, too. They both laughed, and gave up the attempt for a moment as they kissed some more. "Let me do it," she whispered.

"Only if I can watch."

She pulled off her top, unfastened her bra, watched him strip with the same wicked, boyish eagerness that she remembered in him at eighteen. His grin, his open impatience, his rough movements. She began to work on her trousers and he lifted her from the table and ordered, "Now, shimmy." The fabric slid over her hips as she rocked them, and dropped to the floor.

They came together again, skin to skin. He touched her breasts, as if he'd forgotten what breasts were, his hands cupping and caressing, his mouth hot. She felt herself soften and swell even more, every inch of her skin sensitized, aware of itself, full of wanting, ready to burst. Her breasts felt bigger and heavier, her nipples throbbed, her mouth tingled and burned.

He trailed kisses up to her neck, brushed his hands lightly over her nipples, cupped her breasts again, driving her crazy with need.

"I want to feel you," she gasped.

"Now?"

"Yes. Please."

"You don't want—?"

"Not this time. I just want you. Inside me."

She could feel him shaking—not with the adrenaline-rush weakness she'd felt herself earlier but with the vibrating tension of a coiled spring. He was taut all over, so smooth, so warm. She brushed her hand across his groin, felt the instant whiplash of his response and gripped him, loving the way her fingers slipped up and down over the stretched satin skin.

She could have kept going, deliciously distracted by the shape and feel of him, but he nudged her hand aside and sheathed himself with a couple of efficient movements, then turned back to her and anchored his hands on her shoulders.

She wrapped herself tight around him, her calves cushioned against the muscular backs of his thighs, and he pushed to fill her in one long, aching, shuddering stroke. He slid his hands beneath her bottom to lift her a little, to make them fit still closer, then he pulled back and pushed again, even deeper. She gasped at the sensation, and could barely breathe. He filled her completely—different and yet almost a part of her.

She felt pressure and aching and tingling and the world went dizzy. The whole universe turned around this single axis of his body and hers, locked together. She couldn't keep her eyes open, just kissed him wildly and blindly, deeper and deeper, as their rhythm climbed higher. She heard him groan out her name then let her own cries spill out with no holding back.

Her climax shattered around her seconds before his, and the shudders of his release brought a second even stronger wave breaking hard over the first, crashing through her like a surge of ocean crashing on the shore. It was so powerful that it left her without the ability to speak or move for a long time. All she could do was breathe in deep gasps that tore in and out of her like pressured steam.

Jake stood motionless, holding her. Even when he'd eased out of her he didn't let go, just stayed, keeping her warm and balanced on the table—on the *table,* for heck's sake, the one his professional decorator had picked, without a thought in her head as to what it's first use would be.

He spoke before Stacey was ready for the day-to-day reality of words. "The weekend isn't good for me." She could feel his voice vibrating in his chest, against her still-sensitized breasts.

He sounded as if he'd had to struggle to be so rational, and she wanted to tell him, You don't have to be. Say sweet, silly things to me that no one else will ever hear. Say nothing. We don't need this.

"No?" she managed out loud, instead.

"I have three scheduled C-sections tomorrow." He began to pull away, and turned his head, looking for his clothes. "So they'll all need monitoring over—"

"Jake?" she cut in. She hugged her arms around herself, feeling suddenly cold, still perched on the polished surface of the elegant table. She slid her feet to the floor, where the soft pile of the rug welcomed her toes.

"Mmm?"

"I don't think I'm ready for an obstetric discussion just yet." She watched as he picked up his underwear and jeans.

Holding them in front of his body, he looked at her. "It's getting late, Stace. I know you don't want to keep the sitter for too long. I'm trying to—" he waved a vague hand "—help you get home fast."

"I don't need to get home that fast."

"Okay. We'll work things out in a minute, then."

"I mean, I appreciate—"

"It's okay."

Her heart sank. This was beginning to sound like one of her conversations with John. Interruptions and misunderstandings, apologies and missed connections. "I just wanted you to hold me for longer, that's all," she said.

He muttered something under his breath, dropped his jeans and reached her in less than a second. They hugged desperately, like lovers about to be parted by war. "Stace," he muttered in her ear, "I don't know what I'm doing with this sometimes. I'm trying to get it right. Can you cut me some slack?"

"Of course."

"I want to see you on the weekend, and I don't think it's going to happen, and that's burning me up. I'm trying to work something out."

"It's going to burn me up, too. You burn me up. Always."

"Next week? Evenings? I'm free for most of them."

"So am I." Although she questioned the word free, after she'd stopped speaking. Free but wiped, usually. Craving adult conversation but struggling to string two words together if a friend called to talk. Toys not tidied away. Laundry to fold.

She felt wiped, now, and realized that Jake was right about the lateness of the hour. She had to get home and call a cab for Brittany, fill in permission notes for Max and Ella because the day-care center was going on a field trip tomorrow. That's right, she was supposed to provide a packed morning snack for them to take, also.

"Monday night?" she said, because even four days felt like too long.

She suddenly felt a little scared about how much she'd already begun to count on this. She'd begun to count on the secret joy of thinking about him, because sometimes with toddler twins your thoughts were the only thing you really had to yourself. She'd begun to count on the anticipation of seeing him again.

She'd simply begun to count on *him*, to trust him and feel safe with him.

So fast.

How had it happened so fast? Was it only because of the emotional past they'd shared?

Because of what he'd said about saying Anna's name, and because he'd apologized for pushing Stacey away?

"Monday would be great," he said.

He made a second attempt at getting dressed, and this time she didn't stop him but gathered her own clothes and put them on with fingers that still felt more ready for sensual touching than for this practical task.

"My place, this time," she suggested.

"When does John have Max and Ella next?"

"Eight days from now."

"Does he always drive down to collect them?"

"We take turns. I'm driving them north, this time, and he'll bring them home Sunday afternoon."

"So if I came up with you, I could help with the driving and we'd have the whole weekend."

"Oh, wow, that sounds good! Except that I usually leave pretty early, sometimes at three, so that I can settle the twins in at John's by the time he gets home from work. I'll work Wednesday and Thursday next week instead of Thursday and Friday, so we can leave direct from home. But you probably can't get away until later." She pressed her fingers to her temples, trying to get her head around all the complications, the decisions and arrangements that had to be made.

"I can try to switch my hours around," he offered. "But I can't promise. Would it be terrible if we had to leave after five?"

No. It would not be terrible. Because she would be with him.

Chapter Ten

"Ready?" said Jake at the door of Stacey's house, after their initial greeting. They'd smiled at each other, but they hadn't kissed and Stacey was a little shocked at how much she craved the reassurance of just one touch, just one moment.

He was half an hour late and she had already been packed and waiting with the twins ten minutes early, so, yes, she was well and truly ready, but she suspected he had probably moved mountains to make himself free by the middle of a Friday afternoon, so she simply nodded and turned to call the twins.

She had put on one of The Wiggles music

DVD to entertain them while they waited, and could hear them happily yelling, "Wake up, Jeff!" in the other room. As usual, they were totally caught up in the recorded action, as Purple Wiggle Jeff once again fell asleep over his keyboard.

"This is their gear?" Jake asked, indicating the large overnight bag and crammed diaper bag sitting in the front hall. "I'll take the bags to the car and then shift their car seats, if you can unlock your car for me, while you bring the kids out."

"We could have gone in my car and kept the seats where they were. I should have thought."

"Well, I do like my car…"

As well he might, since it was a very expensive and almost brand-new SUV. With the possibility of snow in the forecast farther north, Stacey didn't push the idea of leaving the car seats where they were, and was privately glad that they'd be traveling in such a sturdy, reliable vehicle.

They'd seen each other twice this week. Monday night and Wednesday, both times at her place. It just seemed to make more sense to do it this way. Her regular sitter was still out of action, first with a sprained ankle and now a winter flu virus. She didn't like to get a sitter too often during the week, anyhow, especially if she'd been at work and the twins hadn't seen her all day.

Both evenings had been…mixed.

She had to admit it, as she went through to turn off the DVD. The twins weren't happy about saying goodbye to The Wiggles, so she told them cheerfully, "We'll bring it with us to watch on the weekend with Daddy," which nipped their protests in the bud.

There had been some satisfying stretches of connection and warmth with Jake on Monday and Wednesday nights. And there'd been other stretches where chaos happened, and crying, and mess, and promising conversations evaporated in the face of twin-orientated distractions. Jake always had long days at the hospital, and it was much harder to keep the double or triple conversational tracks going when they were both tired.

On Wednesday, she hadn't been able to get the twins to go down at their normal bedtime. They'd napped for almost three hours at the day-care center, Nancy Allen had told her, and they just weren't tired. But Stacey had known that Jake was waiting patiently for her downstairs. He'd been…well…adorable… playing with Ella and Max for an hour after their baths, but by that time he'd had enough, she could see.

He'd wanted peace and quiet.

And her.

And lovemaking.

And, oh, she'd wanted all this, too, as much as he did, but the more she'd tried to hurry the twins into settling down, the more rambunctious they'd become, and in the end she'd had a choice between leaving them crying with angry frustration in their cribs, and bringing them back downstairs.

She'd made the wrong choice.

She'd lost it, basically. Had given in to her fatigue and impatience and the headache rapidly tightening around her scalp.

"Here, books," she'd snapped at them, throwing a couple into each crib. "Now read, and then sleep." She'd wound up their musical mobile for the fourth time, her fingers rough and impatient on the turn key.

The mobile played "Lara's Theme" from *Dr. Zhivago*. Stacey had always loved that song, but she must have heard it around, oh, nine million times since John's mother had given the mobile to the twins when they were just a month or two old, and she'd begun to have deranged fantasies about upending Max's messy dish of uneaten spaghetti from dinner onto the top of Omar Sharif's exotically handsome 1960's movie star head.

Already regretting her loss of control, she'd managed to take two steps out of the room, and the imaginary spaghetti had slurped down onto the shoulders of the imaginary Omar's enormous Russian military coat when she heard an ominous thud from behind her, followed by loud crying.

It had happened.

Ella had learned to climb out of her crib.

She hadn't yet learned to land safely on the other side.

Hmm. Wednesday night, in fact, hadn't been so much mixed as more of a total disaster.

Carrying Ella out to the car, where Jake had just buckled her seat in place, she kissed the top of her daughter's little blond head and murmured, "You won't be two forever, will you, sweetheart? And I won't be surprised if you climb a few mountains when you grow up. I'm going to be incredibly proud of you."

When she got back to Max, he'd helpfully removed The Wiggles DVD from the player for her, by pressing all the buttons at random, and it was now covered in something sticky that he should not have had on his fingers because surely she'd washed them only fifteen minutes ago. She smelled them.

Ah.

Granola bar.

The one Ella had recently lost somewhere in the vicinity of the couch, she guessed.

"Let's wash hands again," she said. There could still be a rogue piece of granola bar lurking in the room waiting for its next opportunity, but she would deal with it when she got back from Olympia tonight.

Only ten minutes later, they were ready to leave. Twelve minutes, if you counted Stacey remembering she'd forgotten to lock the back door and having to run back inside.

Jake drove. "I brought a picnic," he said as they reached the interstate.

"A *picnic?*"

"I know you don't like the kids to have too much cheap junk food."

"Yeah, the expensive junk food is much better for them. Jake, it's pouring with rain."

"Which is why this is going to be a picnic in the car. This vehicle has all these whizzbang pull-down trays and pullout cup holders that I'm busting to try out."

"Your previous vehicle didn't?"

He shrugged. "I had a classic Jaguar that I sold in Seattle a month before I moved here."

"Quite a switch. Jag to SUV."

"I'm hoping to head up to Mount Hood on weekends for some skiing, or hiking in summer. Decided it was time to pick a sensible set of wheels."

"You really like to keep fit, don't you? Cycling, skiing, hiking." She shifted in the passenger seat so she could look at Jake while he drove.

His profile looked steady, filled with quiet authority. He glanced in the rear vision mirror, changed lanes, increased speed with smooth expertise. In his face she could still see the remnants of the young man he'd once been—he'd shown more vulnerability back then, more edgy teen emotion—but she realized that everything that had happened to him since that difficult time had served to make him confident and assured. Now, even at first glance, he looked like one of life's winners.

"It's the only body I've got," he said. "You know, when I bring a baby into the world, it's almost always so perfect."

"Ten fingers, ten toes."

"And everything works. Lungs and muscles and skin. It's a gift most of us are given, and too many of us—" He stopped suddenly. "I'm sounding so preachy."

"It's okay. I'll overlook that. I'm interested."

So help me, I'm interested in any and every word that comes out of your mouth, Jake Logan.

"Too many of us don't cherish the gift," he said. "That's all."

"Which brings us back to the junk food. I'm still skeptical about the picnic idea."

"You wait. It'll be cozy."

"Cozy?"

"The heating is great in this thing. I'll keep it running. Cozy as a warm blanket by the fire."

"Tosy!" said Ella. "Tosy! Tosy!"

"Tosy!" Max echoed.

"See? They're with me on this."

"While I'm yet to be convinced."

They stopped after an hour, at a scenic layover just off the interstate. "I mean, it would be scenic," Jake insisted, "if we had any visibility."

"The raindrops racing each other down the windscreen will have to count as our distant vista," Stacey agreed.

"Distant and ever-changing. They're turning to sleet."

"Tosy!" Ella said.

"Right on, Terrible Two," Jake agreed, before

exiting the SUV to perform some mysterious action beneath the vehicle's temporarily raised hood, that involved something wrapped in foil which he promised would make sense soon.

Weirdly, it *was* cozy, sitting here with the sound of the rain-slash-sleet on the metal roof. He'd brought three insulated flasks, one filled with creamy potato soup, one with hot chocolate and one with coffee. He and Stacey pulled down trays, flipped open cup holders, and poured hot fluids into insulated plastic mugs.

While they waited for the soup to cool a little, the twins snacked on pieces of fruit or vegetable stuck into individual servings of dip. Apparently apples and Middle Eastern hummus went together a lot better than their mother would have thought. Jake tried it but didn't share the twins' taste.

Stacey sipped her soup, but it was still too hot for the twins.

"That's okay," Jake said, "because we should wait for the hot rolls."

"Who is bringing us the hot rolls?"

"Me. I'll go check 'em." He opened the door of the SUV once more.

"*That* is what's in the foil? And you're sitting the whole package on the engine to warm them up? Jake…!"

He grinned. "Back in a sec."

She couldn't keep the smile from her face. There was really only one word for this whole unique experience that Jake had provided with such flourish.

Tosy.

Twenty minutes later, when they'd finished dips and vegetables, soup and rolls, coffee and hot chocolate and miniature French fruit-and-custard tarts, the sleet turned to snow.

"We still have an hour of driving, Jake."

"I know." He began to pack everything away, sparing narrow-eyed glances through the front windscreen at regular intervals. Stacey helped, sharing his growing concern.

The snow was thickening fast, and darkness had almost fallen.

"It's not settling yet," he said.

"That's something."

"We'll get to Olympia safely, and we'll head straight back. It won't last."

"It shouldn't. I mean, this part of Washington State does not do massive dumps of snow!"

The rest of the drive was an uneasy one, but both Jake and the vehicle handled the conditions well, and they arrived safely at John's just as he pulled into the driveway after his commute home from work. Stacey could see him at the wheel, frowning when he saw the unfamiliar SUV parked in the space next to the garage. He pressed the automatic door opener, eased his car into the garage and appeared a moment later, still frowning. Finally, he recognized Jake, and only then looked across at the passenger seat to see her sitting there. In the backseat, the twins were almost hidden.

"Pull in beside me," he instructed Jake. "There's plenty of room. Don't get the twins wet."

Jake nodded and reversed, then nosed forward into the remaining space. Climbing out, he went to the rear of the vehicle to unload the twins' bags. John leaned in to unstrap Ella, while Stacey unstrapped Max.

"Is your car in the shop?" John asked. The click of the release button punctuated his question.

"No, but the SUV made more sense, don't you think? In these conditions?"

He nodded, and left the issue alone, but Stacey could see he was still unhappy. She felt like a parent trying to promote harmony between two feuding siblings. Now, kids, you have to learn to *share*.

She felt like the monkey in the middle—the one who'd have to explain each man's moods and motivations to the other, keeping conflict to a minimum. Because if *she* didn't promote harmony and help their interactions to run smoothly, who would? The responsibility daunted her, but if there was another choice, she couldn't see it.

"Are you staying for a while?" John asked.

"I think we'll head back," she answered quickly. "If the weather gets worse…"

He gave a short, approving nod, and she could see the relief in his eyes.

Jake hung back politely while she and John got the twins settled in. There was always too much to say, a whole slew of detail about things like where Ella and Max were up to in their potty training—not very far along—and what they liked best for breakfast this week. She had a nagging feeling that she'd missed something, but couldn't think what it was. Finally she hugged them, with her usual struggle to find the right balance between communicating her love and appearing relaxed.

Back in the SUV, as Jake drove down the street, her feelings were mixed. Would John be vigilant enough? That's right! That was what she'd forgotten! She should have told him about Ella climbing out of the crib.

Pulling her cell phone from her bag, she

called him quickly and told him about Wednesday night. "She hasn't done it since, and Max hasn't managed it yet. I think they'll be fine if they're tired, but don't try to put them down before they're ready."

"Oh great, the next fun stage in their development," John groaned. "Wanna come back and collect them again?"

Sometimes, yes, she did.

Oh, but it felt good to be sitting here beside Jake, after she'd ended the call to John, just the two of them wrapped in the cocoon of the dark, warm car.

"Can't make up it's mind, can it?" he commented as they hit the interstate. "Rain or sleet or snow."

"Either way, it's nasty."

"It is."

"I don't mind if you drive slow. We're in no hurry."

He nodded and eased off the gas and they stayed silent for several minutes, with just the rhythm of the wipers going to and fro. Slush gathered near the bottom of the windscreen then slid away across the night-darkened glass.

"Why did you marry him?" Jake asked, out of the blue.

At first it seemed like such a terrible

question. Jake hadn't even used his name. Just "him." Although to be fair, Stacey knew at once who he meant! She almost protested, and had to bite back the defensive answer that first sprang to mind. After a deep breath, she said, "Because I thought there was a good chance that we had the right kind of love."

"But it faded?"

"It was never there, as things turned out. Not the way it needed to be."

"Just a physical attraction?"

"No…no. That part was…" How did you have a conversation like this? "…probably not as strong as it should have been." And, yes, Jake, I'm making a direct comparison between him and you. "As strong as it needed to be," she corrected quickly, although the revised wording wasn't much better.

"Right," Jake said.

She waited but he didn't add anything further, so she took another breath and prepared to speak, needing to make it clearer for him. "My friend Suzanne—she majored in Fine Arts at college and she's an art museum curator now. She's divorced. We're in a similar situation. I'll tell you how she expressed it to me once."

"Go ahead. I'm listening." He didn't take his eyes from the wet road.

"She said to me something like, 'What would you do if you found a beautiful painting on sale at a junkyard for a couple of dollars, and you recognized the artist's name and you knew it would be worth hundreds of thousands of dollars if it was genuine? You think it could be genuine, but it could also be a fake. Do you not buy it, just in case? Of course not. You snap it up because it looks good and it's right there in your grasp, and you authenticate it later, at your leisure.' Well, as Suzanne did, I snapped up the marriage because it looked good and it was right there in my grasp, only when I authenticated it later, at my leisure, it turned out not to be genuine. Does that make any sense?"

"Some."

"With you, I'd had such certainty. It was so overwhelming, and then it went so wrong. We hurt each other so much, Jake, you and I. I wasn't sure I wanted to go through that again. I wasn't sure that I *could*. With John, the fact that it was never overwhelming, never as dangerous…in some weird way that felt like a better foundation. Or I theorized that it was going to be a better foundation. Safer. More rational. On paper it all looked so good."

"And he loved you, presumably."

"He thought he did. We both made similar

mistakes. John's the kind of man—and it can be a heroic quality, so I shouldn't knock it—who totally goes after what he wants. Except that sometimes he goes after it before he's given himself enough time to work out if he really does want it."

"The 'it' in this case being you."

"Me. And children. I wanted them—I'd always wanted them—so he wanted them, too, and we started trying right away. It didn't happen after a year, so he pushed for the fertility treatment before I was fully ready. I would have given it longer, taken some nice vacations together, tried to relax about it, because the tests we had couldn't pinpoint a clear cause."

"That's often the case."

"But he pointed out that we were both getting older. His biological clock was ticking louder than mine. We got onto that whole treadmill of hormone injections and doctor visits and didn't notice how much trouble our marriage was in until, hey presto, we had twins! At which point John did some of the thinking he should have done while we were trying to get me pregnant and discovered, oops, this is a real challenge, maybe I didn't really want it, after all. He began to have the same response to our marriage and it just…fell apart."

"And yet he still takes Max and Ella every second or third weekend."

"He's a good, decent man that way. He would never shirk his responsibilities, or deprive his kids of a father. I'm not sure that he enjoys it much, but it'll be easier for him when they're older. He'll be a great sports dad."

Swish, swish, swish went the wipers after Stacey finished speaking.

Jake knew he should say something, but nothing felt right.

He was stunned at Stacey's sense of honor, at her honesty, at the amount of strength she showed, at the way she could sketch out her ex-husband's character so accurately in just a few strokes, without shooting him down in flames.

"Thank you for telling me," he told her at last. The words felt clumsy and inadequate, even though they were true.

"Early birthday gift," she said lightly. "For Christmas, you can have a blow-by-blow account of my pregnancy symptoms, labor and delivery."

"You're too generous, Handley. You don't have to spend that much on me."

"But I want to, Logan. You're worth it."

"Nah. I'm not. All you're getting from me is a twenty-dollar gift certificate from the book-store at the mall."

Hearing her breathy gurgle of laughter, he glanced sideways and saw the way she was watching him. Her blue eyes were bright and soft, and her cheeks had turned pink in the co-cooning warmth of the SUV. She hadn't taken off her padded pink jacket when they got back in the vehicle after delivering the twins, and it's feathery fake fur collar stood up and made a pale halo around the back of her head.

"Are we joking, Jake, or is there a subtext, here?" she asked him quietly.

There was a subtext.

Definitely.

But he didn't want to admit to it.

How could he tell her how scared he was that he'd end up skimping on what she deserved from him? If John always went after what he wanted before he was sure that he wanted it, Jake had a history of doing the opposite. He was so afraid of ending up with baggage that might make him unhappy that he left all sorts of precious things behind.

He did it every time he moved on, he realized, with a blinding jolt of understanding.

He'd sold his very nice European bicycle just before he left Australia, instead of shipping it to the U.S., and in consequence hadn't cycled for three years because he hadn't made the effort to buy another one until now. He lived in a house furnished like a display window in a homewares store because he'd never collected any mementos from his travels.

Why hadn't he kept the classic Jaguar for tooling around Portland in the summer, and simply bought the SUV in addition? He could afford it. Would ownership of two cars at once have tied him down that much?

"Can I get back to you on the subtext?" he said to Stacey, knowingly trading on her capacity to understand and forgive. She would let it go, give him the right space, trust his intentions, he knew she would.

Sure enough, she told him, "Take your time," and he breathed easy again, while burning with a need to give Stacey at least a part of what she deserved from him.

"Let's stop somewhere for supper," he said. "That picnic is starting to feel too small and too long ago. I'd like to take you somewhere nice."

"I'm not dressed for somewhere nice." She looked down doubtfully at the dark, snug-fitting trousers and soft, finely knit sweater she wore beneath her dusty pink snow jacket.

"You look great." He added, "You always look great." She thanked him and he felt like a heel. He'd meant every word of the compliment, but he might not have said it if he wasn't trying to make up for the secret pond slime part of himself that she still hadn't guessed at.

He knew Stacey.

She would not be sitting in this vehicle with him tonight if she hadn't already made some kind of serious emotional commitment to their relationship, while he couldn't promise himself he had the inner capacity to take it beyond the end of next week, with the responsibilities it entailed.

"I'd love to stop somewhere for supper," she said. "Somewhere quiet, with good service and great desserts."

He knew a place that fit the bill. Dad had taken him there the night after New Year's a few weeks ago, along with Ryan and Scott, to celebrate his return to Portland. They'd had a good evening, reestablishing connections and laughing at old jokes. He hadn't seen his father and stepmother since that evening, although they'd called each other a couple of times.

He knew they'd returned from their visit to his brother L. J. in New York, and intended to drop by their place soon, so he could mention his cousin Jillian, and the potluck dinner, and see how the subject went down. Did Dad still hold out any hope of a reconciliation with

Uncle Terrence? Did he want one? Or was Jillian pushing for an unattainable and unwanted goal?

He found the restaurant without difficulty, and the place was as quiet as Stacey had wanted. They were shown directly to a corner table and given the extensive menu. "A salad will be enough for me," Stacey decided. "And the dessert menu afterward!"

Jake convinced her to share a small carafe of white wine, also, and ordered a seafood appetizer for himself. He enjoyed watching her relax. She'd looked a little tight around the mouth earlier. As they waited for their order, she touched her hand to her hair then told him, "I'm going to freshen up a little. My hair is a bird's nest, right?"

"The waiter grabbed a couple of feathers out of it while you weren't looking. I didn't want to say anything."

She chuckled. "You make me laugh."

That's right, Stace, and I think I need to do it more often.

Even in the humor department, he realized, she used her wry, zany sense of comedy to make others laugh more frequently than she laughed herself. She gave far more than she ever took from anyone.

When she returned from the bathroom, her hair was restored to its usual sheen around her face and her shoulders looked looser. But when she sat down, he told her, "You give too much, Stacey."

"Seriously, the twenty-dollar gift certificate from the bookstore is fine. I'll give you one, too. I won't really do the labor and delivery story, I promise."

"Seriously—I'm the one who's saying seriously now, okay?"

She schooled her face into exaggerated listening mode. "Yes, Dr. Logan."

"I'm just wondering what you do for *you*, that's all."

"Oh, is this part of the rut thing? No, Jake, don't throw the napkin at me. I think I'm okay, is what I'm saying." She leaned forward, struggling to express her meaning. "I know things are a little stressful sometimes, with Max and Ella. If you're talking about Wednesday night, yes, sometimes I have a bit of a meltdown, but a good night's sleep or a rented DVD gets me back on track again."

"It's not enough."

"Most parents of two-year-old twins don't get enough of a break. You get through it."

"Let me spoil you. Can we do that? Every

weekend when John has the twins, please, please let me spoil you, Stace, and take care of you a little bit?"

Their wine arrived, and she smiled at him across the table with a quizzical expression on her face that said she wasn't quite sure what he was promising. Spoil her? When John had the twins? Take care of her? How?

He would have clarified the matter for her, only he realized that he didn't know what he was promising, either.

Chapter Eleven

Jake's house was dark and silent when they entered via his garage. He flicked some switches to bring up the lights, and turned the heating higher. Mmm, it was a little chilly in here, Stacey realized. She gave an involuntary shiver.

The next moment, his arms wrapped around her. "Need some warming up?" he whispered.

"You got a plan for that?"

"Well, there are a couple of nice, strong heating vents I like to stand over. Or..." He trailed off.

"I think I'll take *or*."

"*Or* is always good. I'm especially good at

it in a warm room. Or on a warm carpet. Or in a steaming hot shower. How long since you've been in a hot tub?"

"Uh, let's think… They're not recommended for pregnant women."

"You haven't been pregnant for over two years."

"Which means it must be over three years since I've done that."

"That long! You see?"

She gave a helpless sigh. "You're right. I could do with some spoiling. But I think I've forgotten how it happens."

"It starts with you closing your eyes…"

"Jake, you don't have to—"

"Just let me do this, okay?" he pushed a strand of hair back from her forehead, then leaned down to plant a soft kiss on her mouth. She felt his strength like a column of pure heat. "I want to. We have the whole night."

"The whole night. Oh, that sounds so good!"

"Close your eyes."

He brushed the tips of his fingers down her face and her lids instantly fell. She stood there, smiling helplessly as she waited. "Keep them closed," he whispered. She felt the tantalizing brush of the ball of his thumb across her lower lip. Then he scooped her into his arms and carried her to the couch in his great room. "I'm going to put on some music and go fill the tub. Is there anything you want? Hot chocolate? Do you need a blanket?"

"I'm fine."

"Don't move until I tell you."

She heard the smoky voice of a female jazz singer coming through the surround-sound amplifiers, and could have believed herself in a nightclub, the sound quality was so good. Upstairs, she heard water begin to run, and her body relaxed as if Jake had already lowered her into the steaming water.

Note to self, she thought, take hot baths more often, after the twins are in bed.

Realistically, she knew it probably wouldn't happen. Twenty tiny distractions would fritter the time away and she'd end up deciding it was too much trouble.

Only a few minutes—lazy, dreamy minutes— seemed to pass before Jake came back. "Put your arms around my neck," he said.

"Is it filled already?"

"It's close to full. It fills fast. And I think you dozed for a little while."

"I think I did. I think I'm still asleep. You're only a dream."

"Pinch me. I promise I'm real."

"If I'm dreaming, I'm supposed to pinch myself. Isn't that how it works?"

"So maybe I'm the one who's dreaming…." He nuzzled the top of her head, her temples and her cheek. He brushed her mouth with his lips but didn't seal the kiss. She was left drowsily wanting more, with the delicious scent of his skin and his soap in her nostrils.

Her eyes still closed, she felt him climb the stairs. Her body bounced slightly in his arms, but his breathing was only a fraction heavier than usual with the effort. In the bathroom, he placed her on her feet and she felt heat and steam before she finally opened her eyes to vision that blurred a little.

The water still gushed into the foaming spa, and the bathroom heater high on the wall radiated glowing warmth. The bath mat beneath her feet felt soft and thick. With smooth, unselfconscious movements, Jake began to undress and Stacey did the same. They took sly glances at each other, and smiled when they caught each other at it. "Awake again?" he asked.

"Awaker by the second."

He took her hand and they stepped into the sunken spa together. It came to her thighs when she stood upright, and the water was so hot at first touch that her scalp tingled and the tiny hairs on her body stood on end. Jake sank back into the foam and pulled her down with him and she half floated, half lay in his arms, in no hurry and totally content.

"How are we doing with this so far?" he said softly.

"So far? Is there more?"

"Only if you want."

"I want. Oh, I want… We're doing great."

She wound her arms around his neck and pressed her cheek against his, loving how right it felt, loving the blurred boundary between the tender warmth of the care between them and the powerful heat of the passion. There was no cutoff point. What she felt was seamless—love and friendship and aching desire shading into each other like colors in a rainbow. It had never been this way with John.

If I lose this man…

She pushed the thought away, ready to trade any pain and failure in the future for the bliss she felt now. She'd cross any of those bridges when she came to them, because denying herself now wouldn't lessen any hurt later on, not even a fraction. She kissed Jake, her movement instinctive and totally giving, her body pressing closer as he deepened the contact between their two mouths.

He pushed away from the spa's edge, taking her with him, and they floated together in the middle of the hot, churning pool. She wrapped her legs around him and lay back against the water and he ran slippery, foam-covered hands up her body and over her breasts, teasing her nipples into throbbing life, cupping her fullness, pulling her close again to kiss and suckle her.

He was already fully aroused, nudging hard against her, making her hips rock with willful, impatient need so that she slid against him, back and forth in a slow, snaky rhythm, and drove him wild. "Stop that if you want this to last more than a few minutes," he ground out.

So she pulled back and gripped him with her circled fingers, sliding them in the same pattern as her hips, back and forth, up and down, which drew another shuddering gasp. "Definitely stop *that!*"

"You won't let me have any fun, Jake."

"No, because this time it's your turn first." With a caveman's rough haste, he picked her up and rolled her over the curved lip of the spa, onto the thick, clean toweling spread on the floor. It was warm from the radiant heater above and dried her skin almost instantly when Jake wrapped her in it and rubbed the fabric over her body, deliberately slow and teasing with every movement.

The heat dried his back, too. She felt his hot skin as she tried to pull him down to her, but he resisted. "Not yet. Don't move."

She let out a sound of shocked pleasure and then a gasp as he kissed her center. She felt like a rag doll. Boneless. Muscles like whipped cream. Head swirling. Sensation flowing outward from her core like a flood tide.

But as her climax built and surged she needed him closer, wanted his weight and solid strength here in her arms where she could feel it. She reached for him, grabbing and begging and almost sobbing and he slid higher, trailing his mouth over the hot skin of her stomach and breasts, pressing his cheek against hers—that warm, precious fit of skin against skin once more.

"Stacey…"

"Now. Please, now. I need you inside me." She pushed her hips upward to meet him, and they locked together like magnets in one smooth slide that pierced her throbbing ache and turned it into utter fulfillment. He touched her feverishly, kissed her neck and her hair and finally her mouth, his thrusts harder and faster until she lost all sense of her body's boundaries, and their cries mingled together.

Afterward, they lay there on the hot towel without moving, feeling the faint, rumbling vibration from the spa jets beneath their bodies like a massage. The air steamed, joining their bodies together with moisture.

"We have the whole night," Jake finally said. "We don't have to move for hours."

"No..." The whole night. Like Jake, she wanted to keep saying it.

He didn't speak again for at least ten minutes. "Or we could slide back into the spa..."

"Mmm, that sounds good, too." She stretched lazily and they smiled at each other, and didn't make it into bed for another two hours.

Morning came slow and late.

With Jake's body spooned against her back, and his arm nestled over her hip, Stacey sensed the light growing stronger through her closed lids. She listened automatically for the sounds of the twins waking, then realized drowsily that they weren't here, that she was at Jake's, and she could stay like this for as long as she wanted.

Half an hour later, Jake had other ideas.

His still-sleepy touch tickled her as he ran his hands over her side, her stomach, her hips, her breasts, and they ended up making love in a silly, giggly mood that contrasted totally with last night's intensity, but was in its own way just as good. If you couldn't laugh with a man, how could you ever live with him?

It was after nine by the time they went downstairs, Jake in silk pajama pants and a white T-shirt and Stacey in a borrowed toweling bathrobe that he insisted he never wore. It still smelled like him, though, because it had hung in his closet, and as she crossed the front panels over and belted the robe around her waist she felt as if she was wrapping herself in the very essence of him.

Wrapping herself in his love.

The word *love* hadn't been mentioned yet by either of them, but surely it was there in everything they said and did and felt. She was too content to feel the need to speak it out loud just yet.

I love you, Jake.

She would savor the words like a treat to look forward to.

Jake put coffee and toast on and pulled various ingredients from the refrigerator and the pantry. Stacey made scrambled eggs with sides of crispy bacon and grilled tomato. They ate lazily, but then she began to think seriously about Max and Ella and told him, "I'm going to call John, see how everything went overnight."

The announcement stopped his hand midair and he didn't pour the second coffee she'd held out her cup to receive.

"Should you?" he asked, apparently picking his words with care. "I mean, do you really have to? Wouldn't John call if there was anything to report?"

"It's not that I have to. I want to. I don't know if he'd call. He knows I'll usually call him."

He nodded, although she couldn't tell if he was satisfied by her answer. He tilted the coffeepot and the stream of dark brown liquid hit the bottom of her cup with a trickling sound that seemed to emphasize his silence. Before she could ask for the cordless phone, he handed it to her. She keyed in John's area code and number, aware that Jake's gaze was fixed on the unhesitating way her finger moved. Surely he wasn't surprised that she knew the number off by heart?

"John?" she said when her ex-husband picked up. "Hi, it's me."

"They had a good night, you didn't have to check. As I say every time I have them and you call."

"I know that, but I wanted to see how you were doing, too. Which I also say every time you have them and I call. Did Ella—?"

"Nope. Stayed in her crib. So did Max. I took them to the mall and tired them out."

"The mall? Last night?"

"Relax. We didn't stay until closing time. Just had ice cream and ran around and got in trouble for putting our hands in the fountain."

"And today?"

"I'll think of something!"

She resisted the temptation to come up with activity suggestions for him, and to ask what meals he'd planned. Nor did she ask to speak to the twins themselves because it wasn't fair to John. They sometimes got a little unhappy hearing Mommy's voice over the phone when she wasn't around. They were more used to it the other way around, when they were with her and Daddy called them at her place on a Saturday evening. If she disrupted what they were doing now, it could take him a while to get them settled again.

When she ended the call, she discovered that Jake was still paying close attention. Not his fault, since she could have taken the phone into another room to make the call if she'd wanted privacy. Still, there was something about the way he had his face half-hidden behind the cup of coffee at his lips—a wariness or a disapproval he didn't want to show.

Stacey knew she would always prefer honesty from him.

"Problem, Jake?" she asked.

"I just wonder why you had to do that."

"Why I had to call John?" She shrugged. "Because I'm overprotective."

"Admitting to it doesn't excuse it, Stace."

"True, but I'm not sure why you have a problem with it. Shouldn't John be the one to complain?"

"From what I could hear at this end, he did."

"He doesn't think it's necessary. But I'm trying to support him, because I know how lonely—"

"Are you?" he cut in, standing impatiently. The legs of his chair grated on the floor as he pushed them back. "No! I don't think that is what you're doing. You're trying to micromanage his relationship with his kids. That's how it comes across. With the major side effect that it intrudes on the first piece of real time we've had to ourselves since we began seeing each other. Isn't that just as important? No, *more* important, for once, than whether John managed the kids overnight without getting stressed."

"Is that what this is really about? Having time to ourselves?"

"Yes, and it's what it *should* be about! We have to meet each other halfway, Stacey!"

"What do you mean?"

He turned to put his empty cup in the dishwasher. "I don't want to fight about it."

She lifted her chin, aware of her own stubbornness as well as her fears. "Neither do I, but I do want to clear it up."

He let out a sigh as he turned, took her hands and pulled her to her feet. He held her close. "Maybe it's time we talked about what we're each looking for here."

Stacey's heart gave a gigantic, painful thud and she felt as if someone had poured a bucket of hot water all over her. When she tried to make light of the situation, she almost choked on the words. "Is this the start of one of those it's-not-you-it's-me announcements?"

"No. *No!*" He kissed her, urgent and impatient at the same time, and she responded at once, because kissing him always felt like the most natural thing in the world. They were clumsy together, their timing all wrong. He missed her mouth. Their noses bumped. His hair tickled her cheek.

Finally, still flooded with a shaky relief that this wasn't his breakup announcement, she captured his face between her hands and made the kiss into the sweet one she needed, softening her mouth over his, letting him feel the delicate lap of her tongue.

"Then what's the problem?" she whispered, looking into the green depth of his eyes. "Tell me what this is about, Jake."

"I think we have some parameters to work out. Some details to trade with each other on how we see this."

"This relationship?"

"Yes."

"Okay, then. Spit it out." She rubbed her nose across his and smoothed the lines on his forehead with her thumbs, dared to smile at him.

"Spit it out?"

"Tell me how you see this relationship. Its details and its parameters."

And make it the same as my beautiful picture, please, because if our pictures are too different...

Her relief had faded now. *Parameters* wasn't a good word. *Details?* Not brilliant, either.

* * *

Jake pulled back a little so he could see Stacey's face, and her body language. Her shoulders hunched as she watched him in return, and she folded her arms across her front. Her eyes narrowed and her jaw tightened. She looked defiant and ready to challenge him.

Beyond this, he could see something else.

She looked scared.

The same way I feel...

He had strategies for situations like this. He was a doctor, after all. You never let a patient see that they'd scared you with their symptoms. They didn't need emotion from you, they needed authority and competence and control, and he could do all of that in his sleep, whether it was Stacey wanting his take on their relationship, or a woman in prolonged labor who needed an urgent C-section so that her baby would survive.

"I want more weekends like this one," he said. "I know that, first off." He ran his hands down her arms, but they stayed wrapped, didn't unfurl to touch him.

"So do I." Her voice was low.

She met Jake's gaze and he felt raw, not competent or in control at all. A part of him just wanted to run, to avoid this scene altogether and magically get back to a place where everything was okay, where they didn't need to *negotiate* like this, and could simply let everything unfold at its own pace.

He knew it was impossible.

Because she had kids.

"I'm wondering if that's the best way to handle it," he said.

"If what?" She frowned, not following his line of thought.

"The weekends. If you were right in what you implied when you first came over here with the twins two weeks ago. I'm thinking it's best if we only see each other when Ella and Max are with John."

"What? Did I ever—?" Instantly, she was indignant.

"You said I didn't know what I was letting myself in for," he cut in, "and I'm admitting now that you were right. It's…hard, Stacey. These are another man's kids. You've talked about it yourself, in relation to the idea of John dating again. It's not a casual involvement that I can pick up and drop at will."

"I'm not suggesting that, am I?"

"Of course you're not. But there's a choice that has to be made. To make a commitment to Max and Ella, or to stay at a safe distance from their lives. It's not something I can blow hot and cold over. There's no gray area. It's too important for that. I could hurt them. I could hurt you. I could hurt—" he took a breath that wasn't quite steady, and hoped she wouldn't pick up on it "—myself." He went on quickly, "And I don't want anyone to get hurt over this, least of all two innocent kids."

"So you're choosing the safe distance? You're making that choice on behalf of all four of us?"

"Yes."

She looked very angry now. "How are we going to work it? Pretend that each other doesn't exist for the twelve to twenty days between John's weekends?" She gave him a hard look. "Do you want this relationship at all?"

"Of course I want it! How can you doubt that?" He tried to kiss her but she fought him away.

A sound like a whimper escaped from her throat and it gave him a sense of strength and hope. She couldn't walk away. They both wanted each other too much, didn't they? It ached in him and burned him up every minute he was with her, and most of the minutes when he wasn't, and he *knew* she felt the same because he knew her so well. She would not be here now, and she would not have spent the night with him, if she wasn't every bit as twisted up over this as he was.

And yet she wouldn't kiss him.

He brushed his cheek against hers, tried to find her mouth, but she pressed her lips tight together, closed her eyes and turned her head away. He tried harder, caressing the soft hair he loved, capturing the clean line of her jaw in his palm, whispering to her and kissing her face. She stayed stiff and stubborn, and he couldn't keep pushing for something she didn't want.

"Okay, okay…" he said softly. "We're beyond that, aren't we? We have to work this out, first."

Her eyes flashed open. "You want to know how I can doubt that you want the relationship? Because we're a package deal, Jake, the twins and I! I can't conceive of my life without Ella and Max. I'm not *me* anymore, without them." Her voice went foggy and unsteady, shocking him with its emotion.

"We're not talking about—Stacey, you're making too much of this!" he said on a harsh whisper. He felt a muscle pull in his throat, he was holding himself so tight. "I'm not asking you to deprive yourself of one single hour of the time you spend with your kids."

"No. You're just asking me only to see you on the weekends they're with John. Which means you're asking me to pretend that they don't exist."

"No!"

"You're asking me to pretend, in the context of our relationship, that my children don't exist," she repeated, sounding even angrier.

"Because I don't want to hurt them."

"Because you don't want to hurt or challenge or even, heaven help you, Jake Logan, *inconvenience* your*self* by having a whole, one hundred percent, real relationship. I don't think it's anything to do with hurting them, or hurting me. So tell me just what the hell any relationship between us would mean under those narrow circumstances?"

"It would mean what it meant last night. Time together. Just the two of us. No stress. No distractions. Is that bad?"

"It's not enough! Is that all you're ever going to want? All you're ever going to promise?"

"Should I make any kind of a promise before I know if I can keep it? Isn't that what John did, and then he found that he couldn't?"

"You're not John."

"No, I'm not. That's why we're having this argument, instead of me telling you exactly what you want to hear, the way he did. You've told me that. I'm being honest. Is that wrong?"

Was she even listening?

"Are you waiting for proof, or something?" She shook her head, pressing her fingertips against her temples as if they throbbed. "You're never going to get proof, Jake. Some things you just have to take on faith. And if you can't do that…"

"This is too important for faith."

"No. Faith is the only possibility, when something's this important! I thought you'd warmed to my kids and started to care about them—"

"I have. They're great."

She ignored him. "—and I thought that you were getting to know how to handle them, getting to understand what it meant to have them in your life."

"I am, which isn't fair on them beyond a certain point. And that's why this decision has to be made now."

There was a heavy beat of silence.

"It's already been made, Jake." She turned on her heel, blinking back tears. "I'm getting dressed. You don't have to take me home. I'll call a cab."

Chapter Twelve

Jake was waiting for Stacey at the foot of the stairs when she came back down, dressed in yesterday's clothing. She hadn't showered—had been too upset to spend a second longer than she had to in Jake's house—and felt stale and tired.

"Cancel the cab," he said. "I'll drive you."

"It's fine." She stepped past him, toward the front door.

"No, it's not. We need to—"

"We need to get out of each other's space. I'm angry. And I'm—I'm hurting, Jake. I can't believe you are doing this. Running away.

Again. I can't believe I let you do this to me. For once in my life I wanted a relationship with another adult that would be more than *amicable,* so I ignored all the warning signs. And I knew it would hurt. But I didn't think it would hurt so much, so soon." She practically had to gasp out each word. They were sobs more than words, every one of them jerky and breathy and tight.

"Last night—" he began.

"Last night was so wonderful. All night it was wonderful, lying beside you. It felt so right. It always has. This morning was wonderful. Waking up still touching you. Feeling the heat of your body against mine. But it's not enough, Jake. I can't carve my life into little pieces to fit what you want. These are my kids we're talking about. My children. The most precious, important things in my life. I need courage and faith and promises, and so do Ella and Max. You've told me you can't give me those things. So, no, I'm not canceling the cab."

She looked through the glass panels beside his door and saw the taxi cruise to a halt in front of the house. Any minute, the cab driver would beep his horn. At the edge of her vision, she saw Jake move to open the door for her. He looked white and dry-lipped, and she knew that she could never accuse him of taking any of this lightly.

Instinctively, she wanted to make him feel better, hug him close one last time because even when they were this much at odds with each other, something about their hearts still *belonged.*

She couldn't explain it, even to herself.

He held open the door, silent and struggling. Only as she stepped through it did he finally manage to say, "Call me, Stacey."

"Why? What about?"

"I don't know. Just call."

Helplessly, she gave him one last look but couldn't even say goodbye and neither did he. He just leaned on the door handle as he watched her walk down the steps toward the waiting cab. When she climbed out of it in front of her own house, she felt as stiff and aching in the joints as an old woman.

Inside, she listened to her messages because it was one of those things you did when you walked in your door—one of those things you did when you couldn't summon the will or the organizational skills to do anything else, because all this task involved was the press of a button.

"Stacey?" said Giselle's machine-distorted

voice. "I have some great news for you." There was a pause. "Well, I hope you'll think it's great news. How come you are *never* home when I call, by the way? I'm coming for the weekend. My flight gets in Saturday at 10:05, but don't worry about picking me up, I'll get a cab from the airport. Busting to see you, sis. Call me if you get this message. Don't leave me sitting on your front doorstep without a key, okay?"

Stacey had almost done exactly this.

She checked her watch and realized that if Giselle's flight got in on time she could be here at any moment. It was the last thing she wanted, when she felt like crawling into bed, staying there for hours and cradling the ache in her stomach the way she used to cradle the growing bulge of her babies as they developed inside her.

With a bitter private smile, she wondered what would happen if she cried on her baby sister's shoulder the moment she walked through the door, and realized she couldn't face the possibility that she might spill her heart, with all its anguish and doubt, to Giselle—Giselle, with her perfect life, basking in the warm glow of parental approval.

I have to pull myself together before she gets

here, she knew. I have to bury everything safely inside where she won't see or guess. It's going to be amicable or bust, as usual.

She hurried up the stairs and into the shower, stripping quickly, throwing every garment into the hamper because all of them smelled of Jake and their night together. The hot needles of water washed away some of the stiffness and a tiny bit of the pain. They cleaned up her tears and masked the redness around her eyes.

She'd just found fresh clothing, pulled a brush through her damp hair and disguised the ravages of the morning with a little makeup when she heard the doorbell downstairs.

Showtime.

She went down and opened the door to her sister on the doorstep.

"Oh, Stacey, it's so good to see you!"

Giselle looked as glamorous and beautiful as any trophy wife should. She wore red—a gorgeously cut scarlet wool coat, a darling scarlet felt hat dipped over her forehead, a red cashmere sweater that showed every curve, red leather boots and—just in case the red theme was getting too much—designer blue denim jeans. She enfolded Stacey in a very expensive scarlet hug and—incongruous detail—Stacey felt her tremble a little as she held the contact for longer than usual.

"Are you okay, Giselle?"

"Of course I'm okay." Giselle gave a haughty sniff and marched inside with a shopping bag in one hand and a bulging overnight bag in the other. "Or I will be, when I've had coffee."

"Same here," said Stacey. "I'll put some on."

She led the way toward her kitchen. Behind her, Giselle put her bags down at the foot of the stairs. "Actually," came her voice, sounding very small, suddenly. "That was a lie, just now. I'm not okay, Stacey."

Stacey paused and turned. This was a surprise. Or maybe not. Maybe those answering machine messages over the past few weeks had been just a little *too* perky, even for her sister. "No?" she said gently.

"Major no." She flapped her hands. "I wanna laugh about it. Be cynical. And drawl a lot. So my marriage is over, I'll get the best divorce lawyer in California and take the bastard to the cleaners. And smoke. I wanna smoke soooo bad!"

"You've never smoked," Stacey said blankly.

"I know. Am I too old to start? Wait, I can answer that. I'm too *pregnant* to start."

"Giselle? You're pregnant? That's—!"

Not so wonderful, apparently.

"And I'm crying. And ruining my makeup. Which is *not* from the discount drugstore, let me tell you. Stirling says I've been spending too much. But that's not the issue. He's looking for excuses. Because of the aff—" she couldn't get the word out, because she was crying "—sffair."

"Oh, Giselle. Oh, honey." Stacey wrapped her sister in a much better hug, this time around, and forgot roughly ninety-five percent of the times they'd rubbed each other the wrong way, in the past, or been critical of each other's choices, or fought each other for their mother's approval and Giselle had always won.

"Great surprise weekend visit, huh?" her baby sister said.

"Not for you, but for me it is. I am really glad you came. Actually, Jizzy, I think this is the nicest thing you've ever done for me, to think of my shoulder as the one to cry on. Which doesn't sound like a compliment, does it? But I mean it as one. Hey, let me get us that coffee before I've dug myself so deep in the hole I can't see out the top."

Giselle laughed through her tears. "You haven't dug yourself in a hole. It's true. We haven't been close. I've always felt I had so much to prove to you."

"Prove to *me?*"

"You've lived your own life. You're brave. Me, I'm such a lightweight. Which has suited Mom until now because it means I've never given her any grief."

"You're not a lightweight!"

"I—I don't even know why I picked your shoulder. Maybe because Mom doesn't want to know, and my so-called friends want to wait to find out the size of my alimony payment before they decide whose side they're on."

"That bad?"

"With the friends?"

"With the marriage. With Stirling."

She shrugged. "Think so. Been happening for a while. Since two days after I found out I was pregnant, in fact."

"When was that, honey?"

"Middle of November. I'm starting to show, if you look."

"Oh, lies! You are as flat as a pancake!"

"I'm not." With a wry smile, Giselle took Stacey's hand and guided it to just below the waistband of the designer jeans. "See?" she said softly. "It's a bump, and it's hard. There's a baby in there. I've seen its heartbeat on the sonogram. Isn't that a miracle? Even with

Stirling being such a piece of slime with this chicky-babe of his, it's a miracle."

"It is." Stacey hugged her again. "It's wonderful."

"Only I won't tell you what Mom thinks I should do about it, quoting here, 'if you can't do the work to save your marriage,' unquote."

"Oh, *shoot!*" Stacey said. "You don't have to tell me what Mom thinks you should do about the baby, because she said the same thing to me seventeen years ago, and so I know."

"Oh, Stacey! With Jake? When you were pregnant and there was all that fuss? I never knew!"

"I'm starting to think there's a lot we've never said to each other, Giselle. And speaking of Jake…"

They talked for three solid hours, about Jake and his fear of promises he couldn't keep, about Stirling and his affair, about their mom and dad, and the twins, and John and about fifty other things—some trivial, some important—while sitting at her kitchen table drinking coffee and eating every bit of chocolate Stacey had in the house.

To be honest, Stacey ate most of it, and Giselle ate two apples and a banana, as well, for the baby.

When they were all talked out, they went to

the mall. Several crammed shopping bags later, Giselle got hungry and they discovered it was already dark outside so they went and ate Mexican—"The baby wants Mexican," Giselle insisted, "Lots of Mexican"—and didn't get home until nine o'clock, at which point the baby unsurprisingly wanted heartburn medication.

"And yet, even though we're both miserable, hasn't it been the best day, Stacey?" Giselle said.

"It leaves *amicable* in the dust," she agreed, and when she explained about the unsatisfactory, superficial nature of *amicable,* Giselle completely understood.

"Jake, this is John," said a male voice over the phone when Jake picked it up at four o'clock on Sunday afternoon. "John Deroy."

It wasn't who he'd expected to hear.

"Yeah, hi, John. What's up?" An uneasiness twisted in his gut. All yesterday and all today, he'd been hoping Stacey would call but she hadn't. At least five times, he'd picked up the phone to call her, but then he'd hit a wall.

What would he say?

What had changed?

A part of him thought he had to be the

biggest coward in the world. He should just step up to the plate without even thinking about it, commit himself to Max and Ella like committing himself to home-delivery pizza topping. Mushroom and onion. Done deal. No regrets. No second chances. No significant downside.

But kids weren't pizza toppings.

Stacey was being unfair.

He had to stick to his principles on this. He couldn't make rash promises, couldn't take on the biggest responsibility of a man's life when he doubted, in his heart, that he could live up to it.

Hearing John at the other end of the line, he almost challenged him.

How could you do it, Deroy? How could you push Stacey into something neither of you were ready for, or right for together, without making the effort to step back and work out what you really wanted? We're not talking pizza toppings. Do you know what damage you've done?

He managed to hold the words back, and heard John ask, "Do you have Stacey there, by any chance?" He sounded worried and impatient, and his voice was indistinct, cut across by static and background noise.

"Uh…no, sorry, I don't."

"Because I couldn't get her at home and she's not picking up on her cell. Do you know where she could be?"

"No, can't help you there, either. Is there a problem?"

"Look, don't worry about it. I'm pulled over on the interstate, and there's been an accident somewhere ahead. We're down to one lane, we're crawling and it's wet."

"Wet here, too." Jake could see the gray drizzle and poor visibility through his big windows, and the light had already faded considerably.

"The point is, I'm going to be later getting to Stacey's than I planned, and the twins are getting sick."

"Yeah?" Jake's medical instincts kicked in at once and his level of concern notched up higher. "What's wrong?"

"It's probably nothing. You know, they're always teething, getting a fever for twenty-four hours and then it goes. Max was fretful earlier in the afternoon and he felt a little warm. Ella seemed okay. Now she feels warm, too, and Max is burning up. I wouldn't have started the drive if I'd thought they'd get worse this fast. I didn't even think to bring medication."

"Are you thinking you'll turn back?"

"No, I'm closer to Portland now so it doesn't make sense, but I just wanted to get hold of Stacey, warn her they may need the doctor tonight and make sure she has medication on hand to bring the fever down."

"Any other symptoms? Stomach pain or vomiting? Neck stiffness? Rash? Light sensitivity?"

"I don't know. No vomiting. Neither of them have eaten much today. The other things...I don't know. They don't seem too happy. Listen, I'm going to get going again, because this traffic isn't clearing and it's going to take a while. If you can get in touch with Stacey for me, I'd appreciate it." He had to yell to make himself heard above static and traffic, windscreen wipers, fretful twins and rain. "I left a message on her machine, but there was a lot of distortion. I don't know if she'll be able to make out the message, but I don't want to keep trying while I drive. Not in these conditions."

"Don't worry about it, John. I'll handle it at this end."

"I really appreciate it," he repeated, then ended the call, leaving Jake uncertain about the rising level of his concern.

Two-year-olds with fever, bad driving con-

ditions, crawling traffic, Stacey out of contact.
What did it all add up to? A slow, frustrating
evening? Or something much worse?

He tried Stacey at once but got the same
result that John had. A machine at her house,
and one of those maddening announcements
about her cell being switched off or out of
range. Frustrated at these electronic dead ends,
he grabbed a jacket and his car keys and left the
house. He could go to a drugstore and pick up
some likely over-the-counter medications for
Max and Ella and deliver them to Stacey's. If
she was expecting John soon, she'd surely show
up.

When he arrived at her place, she was already
there. He saw the lighted windows, and
glimpsed her shadow moving. He pressed her
doorbell, not knowing what she'd think when
she saw him standing there, not having a clue
how he felt himself, or where this might end up.

"Jake…" Her face froze instantly into
wariness, and he could practically see her heart
speeding up, thudding in her chest.

Or was that his own heart he sensed?

"Where were you?" he blurted out, as if he had
any rights over the way she spent her free time.

"Taking my sister to the airport," she answered
blankly. "She came for a surprise visit. We had

a really great time together. But what—?" She'd seen the drugstore bag in his hand.

"I have a message for you from John," he said.

"From John?"

"He tried to call you. He left a message on your machine, but thought it might have been too distorted."

"I haven't checked the machine. I only just got home." She went white and sagged against the door. "What's wrong? Why would he call you if—?"

"It's okay. Let me come in."

She moved aside, her body angular and tight and her hand still gripping the door handle like a life raft. "You have to tell me! Is it the twins? Come… Come…" Where? It sounded as if she'd forgotten the rooms in her own house. She circled unsteadily. "Just tell me, Jake."

He stepped forward and held her. Arm around her back. Hand under her elbow. Because he seriously thought she might fall to the floor if he didn't. "They're fine. Well, they have a fever, and John's stuck in traffic on the interstate. That's all, I promise."

"Okay…"

"I picked up some medication for you, and

I'll stay until he gets here and take a look at them if you want."

"He hasn't had them at the doctor? He drove, when they were sick?"

"I think the fever came on more quickly than he expected. Max only got fretful after lunch, apparently. You know what kids are like. And John couldn't have predicted that he'd have such a slow trip."

Bizarre. Here he was, defending her ex.

The argument that had sent her angrily out of his house and into a cab yesterday morning was…not forgotten, exactly. Just biding its time. They'd have to get back to those issues eventually.

She sagged again. Against Jake, this time, not the door. "How long before he gets here? They shouldn't be traveling when they're sick. Did it really only start after lunch, or did he just not pick up on it? How come he's this late?"

"He said there'd been an accident and traffic was crawling. Shouldn't be more than another hour, at this point, let's hope. He was over halfway here."

She nodded. "So I'll just have to wait. Thanks for coming all this way, and for picking up the medication. You didn't have to, Jake."

She took the drugstore bag from his hand and

made a vague attempt at turning him back toward the door. He could easily take the way out she offered, and get back to his own life and the difficult, responsible stuff such as deciding which pizza toppings to commit to this evening, but something in him rebelled.

"No. I'm not leaving yet."

"It's okay. Really. You're right. These things happen. Kids get sick."

Another bizarre reversal. She'd begun to reassure him, instead of the other way around.

"I want to stay until John gets here," Jake insisted. "I want to take a look at them. And I don't want you to have to be on your own while you wait."

"What did he say? How bad does he think they are? What has he said to make you think—?"

"Relax…relax. Is it so incomprehensible that I'd want to stay?" He ran a caressing hand down her back but she turned neatly out of reach before he could make his touch more intimate.

"Promises, Jake?" she said lightly. "Remember? Commitments and responsibilities and taking the bad with the good. You have trouble with all that."

"Don't let's go there right now. This isn't

about whether I should make promises. Or whether I can. It's just about—" He stopped and swore. "I care about you Stacey. That hasn't changed. Let it count for something, even if it's only to help you through one difficult evening."

"I'm sorry, this is making me tense. We didn't part very well yesterday."

"We didn't," he agreed.

They looked at each other helplessly, and he wanted so badly to kiss away the stress and uncertainty he could see in the way she held her mouth, but maybe she'd seen the intention in his face because suddenly she pressed her lips together and turned abruptly away once more. "Do you want coffee, or something, while we wait?"

"Thanks." He followed her into her wonderful, quirky kitchen. The warmth and color enveloped him like welcoming arms. Light bounced off the gleaming porcelain of her teapots and she must have heated cinnamon rolls in the oven for a breakfast treat this morning because he could still smell the mix of spice and yeast. "You said your sister was visiting. How is she?"

He remembered Giselle as vibrant, outwardly sure of herself and spoiled—Trisha Handley's favorite, because she found her younger daughter's priorities and choices so much easier to understand.

"Not so good," Stacey answered. "She has a baby due in six months but her marriage is on the rocks. Which meant for the first time in our lives we had a great time together, because we had some common ground. Doesn't that sound terrible?"

"Sisters in marital misfortune, united against the world."

She winced, and he almost laughed at the endearing way she was so hard on herself, sometimes. "I told you it sounded terrible. I don't expect you to understand…."

"Relax. You'd be unbearable if you were perfect, Stace."

She didn't really hear him, because she was still working out what she felt and what she meant. He wanted to smooth away her frown with his fingers, or his lips. "…but somehow we actually listened to each other this time, and I discovered that from her perspective it wasn't any easier being Mom's favorite daughter than being the one who never did anything right."

"And what did she discover about you?"

"That I care about her, and would so much love to be close. I think we will be, now, even if she patches things up with Stirling-the-Multimillionaire."

"Which you hope she doesn't."

"Not to make us more equal, Jake, seriously, but his financial status was always the best thing he had going for him, and my sister deserves more than a platinum credit card to make her happy. Speaking of patching things up, though, is there any news on your cousin Jillian's quest to bring the family back together?"

"We're taking it slow. I'm planning to test the waters with Dad the next time I see him. The rift was a lot wider and deeper than the one between you and your sister. But hey, how's that coffee coming?" he added quickly, before all this talk of sibling rifts and sibling bonds could remind her of how worried she was about the twins.

"Hmm, it's not, is it?" She grabbed the coffeepot and went to rinse it out.

Jake sat and watched her at work—the neat efficiency of her movements, the way her hair always fell forward when she leaned over a task. His heart twisted painfully as he contrasted what she deserved with what she had, and what he could undertake to give her.

Not much.

Complete attention and devoted spoiling every second or third weekend, and nothing in between.

I want to marry you, Stacey, he rehearsed in his head. *I want to be a second father to Max and—*

Stop right there.

He felt the blind panic setting in sharp and sudden, like a hard frost on a clear winter day. He felt the weight of responsibility like a millstone around his neck, and the possibility of hurt and loss and helplessness looming like the cloud of volcanic ash he remembered from the eruption of Mount St. Helens when he was a child.

What if I'm not strong enough? What if loving Stacey and her kids means never having another day of real happiness for the rest of my life because we've suffered some terrible misfortune and I have to carry the weight of her grief as well as my own? I was only eighteen when Anna died, but what's different at thirty-five? The heart is less resilient as it gets older. The damage would only be worse.

Look at her. She's strong and beautiful and she tries so hard. She deserves more than I can give. I promised to marry her once before, and look what happened. I can't do it to her again.

I can't do it to myself, either.

"I wish he'd get here," she said suddenly. She put her fingers to her mouth and chewed on a nail, and he remembered how she used to do that when her mother would make her feel inadequate about something.

And the nail would get stripped to the quick.

Jake went over to her at the sink. "He'll get here."

He didn't think about it, he just held her, buried his face in her hair and kissed any place he could reach. Ears and neck and forehead. Love burned in him like acid, so strong but doing neither of them any good. She was fabulous and he wasn't good for her, and he couldn't think of any way to change the situation.

"I love you, Stacey," he heard himself say.

"I love you, too, Jake," she whispered back. "And I hate you for making me feel like this."

"I know."

"When's he going to get here?"

"Soon."

"The coffee—"

"Forget the damn coffee." He couldn't help it, he just had to kiss her, pouring everything he had into the contact of mouth on mouth. She kissed him back, lifting her face to meet him, holding him hard, kissing him with her heart more than with her body, giving everything she had.

"I hate you, Jake," she said, dragging herself back. Her voice shook. "I really hate you."

The doorbell sounded.

Chapter Thirteen

"Max feels so hot," John said. He hurried up Stacey's steps with the little boy in his arms. "Feel him, Stacey. I couldn't find the thermometer."

"It should be in the diaper bag." Stacey touched Max's forehead and gave a hiss of shock at its dry heat. His cheeks were scarlet, Jake noted. The child's eyes were glassy and he seemed too silent in John's arms. "Sweetheart, you're feeling real bad, aren't you? How's Ella?" She took her son from John as she spoke. The car had been warm so he was dressed only in corduroy trousers and a turtleneck. "His whole body feels hot."

"I looked in the diaper bag," John answered. "She's not so hot, just listless. She said her tummy hurts."

"The outside pocket. It slips down sideways. Could you please at some point remember to buy your own supplies of this kind of stuff to keep at your place?" Her voice was pitched too high, and when she'd finished speaking, she bit her lip. This was hardly the time to make suggestions to John about greater efficiency in their shared care of the twins. Jake noted the usual double strand in the anxious exchange between the two parents.

"I'll get Ella," John said. "And you can save the critique on my parenting for a better time, Stacey."

"Is there gear to bring in?" Jake asked. He and John hadn't made the effort of greeting each other, they'd simply exchanged wary nods.

"Please, if you can."

"What are we doing?" Stacey came in. "Leave their gear. I want to take Max to the hospital. Both of them."

"The hospital?" John seemed shocked.

Jake took a deep breath. Stacey and John were both all over the place, the failure of their marriage more evident than he'd seen it before.

They hovered on a knife edge of tension and blame and defensiveness with each other, practically biting their tongues every time they spoke. It was up to him to stay in control, he could see.

"Will you let me take a look at both of them?"

Stacey turned blindly in his direction, with Max's hot little head still pillowed limply on her shoulder. "Yes. Please. Yes. Forget about their gear."

"Put him on the couch. Find that thermometer. And grab me a teaspoon?"

He made a quick, professional examination, while she scrabbled in the side pockets of the bag, cursing under her breath. Max's glands were up. Jake used the spoon as a tongue depressor but it was too slippery and Max fought it. The room's general lighting wasn't focused enough, either, so he couldn't get a good look. From the brief glimpse he managed to get, he thought the throat and tonsils looked red.

Temperature was way high. He guessed the reading would hit between 103 and 104 degrees. He switched on the floor lamp beside the couch and Max turned his head away and hid his eyes with his hand, but the reaction wasn't conclusive. Most kids didn't want light in their eyes when they were ill. No neck stiffness, from what Jake could tell, and no sign of a rash, but on the other hand…

"When did you first notice he didn't seem well?" he asked John, who stood in the doorway, holding limp little Ella. She didn't seem like the same child who had catapulted onto Jake's swing set, two weeks ago, a whole ten seconds after discovering it was there.

"Half an hour or so before we set out."

"And he got quickly worse in the car?"

"Yes."

Responsibility kicked him in the gut again. He didn't think this was meningitis or any other potentially life-threatening illness. It could be strep throat, or maybe just one of those nasty, spiking fevers that heralded a common cold and needed to be brought down with medication and tepid water, but if he called it wrong…

I'm too close, he knew. Doctors are told, "Listen to the mother," and Stacey is scared, but I'm picking up on her fear too much. I can't step back. I can't judge this, and I shouldn't let it rest on my opinion.

"Take him to the hospital," he said, and saw Stacey press her hands to her mouth as she nodded. "Just to be on the safe side, Stace. They'll test for strep throat and a couple of other things. They'll have antibiotics on hand."

"John…?"

"Put them back in the car?"

"Yes. Jake, thank you for giving your opinion. Would you be able to lock up before you leave? I—I want to get going right away." Again, she was trying to send him home because he didn't belong.

"Sure. Then I'll follow you to the hospital," he said.

"You don't have to—"

"Please do not tell me that I don't have to come." He controlled his voice with difficulty. "I know that. I'm coming because I want to be there. I know most all of the pediatricians now, and that may help you get answers faster and clearer."

Stacey just nodded, and he was left with no idea where their relationship currently stood. They loved each other. She hated him. They couldn't go forward, and they definitely couldn't go back. He was still so scared about the responsibility and the promises, but he was absolutely flaming terrified of losing her.

In a flurry, she locked the house and jumped into John's car. Jake followed them down the street, seeing the shape of Stacey's head in the front passenger seat and John's behind the wheel. Once or twice she looked in John's direction as if they were talking but far more often she turned around and checked the twins in the rear seat.

It felt so wrong to have her there in her ex-husband's car instead of here with him that Jake felt physically ill.

At the hospital, they went through the usual progression. He rarely experienced it from the perspective of a member of the public and he was torn by another gut-twisting shock at how much he wanted to pull rank, yell at the triage nurse, "No! I'm not a family member, but I am a doctor at this hospital, and I want some medical attention for these kids *now!*"

With Max's fever officially pegged at 104.4 degrees Fahrenheit, he didn't have to pull rank. The twins were both taken in to the pediatric section of the E.R. very promptly. Stacey went with them, while John stayed to fill in the paperwork. He'd parked in a five-minute zone just beyond the ambulance entrance, and they'd been here longer than that already.

"John, I can move your car for you if you'll give me the keys," he offered as John frowned over insurance details.

The other man looked up and his vision cleared. "Thanks. That would be great." There was an awkward pause while they stared at each other. "Look, it's none of my business what happens between you and Stacey," John began.

"It is your business," Jake answered. "You're Max and Ella's father. It's always going to be your business. And believe me, the question of what I owe to their well-being is not something I'm going to overlook, whatever happens."

John nodded. "Yeah, good, because I'll personally rip your guts out with my fingernails if you damage them in any way."

Jake nodded, too. "Right back at you, John."

"Good. So we're clear?"

"Yep. Looks that way."

"Won't be necessary, I hope. The guts thing."

"Not in my plan, for sure."

"Good."

"Right."

They punched each other on the upper arm in a half friendly, half threatening way and strangely enough it felt all right—good enough for them to both break into a slightly shame-faced grin as they realized that they'd shared exactly the same violent Neanderthal fantasies about what they'd like to do to each other in defense of Stacey and everything that was important to her.

"You love her," John said.

"But I don't know what to do about it."

"No. That's always the tough part."

Jake sighed. "Give me your keys and I'll move the car."

When he arrived back in the E.R. waiting room, John had left the admissions desk and gone through. Jake flashed his hospital ID to a nurse who didn't know him and she pressed the door release. "Max and Ella Deroy?" he asked.

She checked her computer screen. "Beds three and four in the pediatric room."

He strode down the corridor. In the doorway, he stopped. You could have painted the scene, a harmonious composition of white hospital sheets, gleaming silver machinery, warm flesh tones and just a few splashes of bright color. John sat hunched in a chair, reading Ella a storybook with a red-and-yellow cover. Stacey leaned toward Max and brushed the hair back from his forehead, her indigo sweater the richest color in the room.

No one had seen Jake yet, which meant he could stay like this, watching his own control unravel like a badly knitted sleeve.

Where could he possibly fit into the picture? To an outsider's eye it was already complete. Two loving parents and two adorable kids. He knew better. He'd seen nothing in John and Stacey's dealings with each other to suggest that their marriage could ever rekindle. Still, it took courage to take on the complexity of a second marriage and a blended family.

"You deserve more, Stace," he muttered under his breath. "You don't deserve my doubts, and this fear that churns me up inside."

Across the corridor, he heard an alarm sound, followed by a flurry of activity. A woman was crying. A doctor yelled for a nurse. Two more doctors strode past, and he heard one say to the other, "Who's going to tell the family?"

Professionally, Jake could handle anything his work threw at him. Personally, he was still running scared, and Stacey deserved so much more than what he could give. He came so close to simply walking out without even catching her eye—he could leave John's keys and a brief verbal message with a nurse—but then he felt a powerful surge of disgust at himself and knew he couldn't do that. He'd at least tell Stacey that he was leaving. Taking a strong, steady breath, he went into the room.

"Here are the keys, John," he said. "The car's in the first visitor lot, second row. The lot should start to empty out soon. It won't be hard for you to find."

"Thanks, Jake."

"Stacey, I'm going to head out of here."

She looked up, taking a second or two to focus on his face. She frowned. "Okay."

He almost launched into an explanation about how he didn't belong and didn't want to intrude, but then realized that this in itself would be an intrusion. Their fractured relationship was the last thing on her mind, right now. When he looked back at her from the doorway, she was stroking Max's hair again.

Outside, the winter darkness had fallen thickly and the air was cold and fresh. It had to be after six by now. He left the hospital and knew he couldn't go home. He headed for his parents' house, hoping his father would be there.

He got on well with his stepmother, Abigail. At forty-four, she was only nine years older than he was. His younger stepsisters were good kids, also. Well, not kids anymore. Suzie was twenty-two and still in college, and Janet was twenty-four.

But it was Dad he needed to see.

Suzie met him at the door, carelessly forking lasagne into her mouth. "Mom's been cooking comfort food, Italian-style, and I'm getting a head start on it. Is that why you're here?"

"No, I'm hoping Dad's around."

"He is. Somewhere. In his study? But have some lasagne anyhow."

"Maybe later, when we're actually supposed to be eating."

"Might not be any left by then. I'll tell Mom you're here."

"I'll be with Dad."

"See you in a bit." She disappeared in the direction of the kitchen, while he headed for the study, where copies of Dad's books and articles held pride of place amid a clutter of research materials that the man somehow never had time to file away.

He found his father checking e-mail with the lights still not turned on because, as often happened, darkness had crept up on him without him noticing. "Let me help you actually see your keyboard, Dad," he drawled as he flicked a couple of switches, and Lawrence Logan blinked and laughed.

"Jake… You know, I still get people writing to thank me for the books, after all these years. I've been trying to reply to this one." He pointed to some text on the screen. "She's had a rough time, from what she says." He stood and engulfed his number two son in a rough bear hug.

"I'm not surprised that you still get letters and e-mails. Some of those self-help manuals go out of fashion pretty fast, but yours have staying power. They weren't about gimmicks. They cut to the heart."

"Too much to the heart, sometimes."

"You're talking about Uncle Terrence."

"It was a pretty humbling lesson for me, Jake, although he's never believed me when I've tried to tell him so. I shouldn't have included his family as a case study, even with the details from several other families mixed in to disguise it and take it in a different direction. I should have realized it wasn't the way to show him how much he'd hurt Lisanne and me."

"You mean the way he rebuffed you when Robbie was kidnapped?"

"We tried so hard to reach out, to help them in their search for Robbie, but no matter what we did, he interpreted everything as my saying, "I told you so," because of the way I'd questioned his priorities."

"He'd questioned yours, too, hadn't he?"

"We never saw eye to eye, even as kids. I thought a missing child should transcend our differences. He didn't. The timing of both my books was bad, from his and Leslie's perspective. When *The Most Important Thing* came out, they had a false lead on his whereabouts that same month. While my book was selling its way up the charts, they were chasing a mirage, with their hearts freshly bleeding. Your mother and I tried to reach out. Again. And again we got the door shut in our faces. And the first week that *Hardest to Forgive* hit the *New York Times* Bestseller List, your brother had just gotten his driver's license and brought his first serious girlfriend home to meet us."

"He and Robbie are almost the same age," Jake realized. "I guess they kept thinking Robbie should be with them, reaching those same milestones. Dad, it sounds as if you'd still like to heal the breach. Have Scott or Ryan talked to you about any of this lately?"

"You mean your cousin Jillian's good intentions?" A sour tone entered his voice.

"Yes. You heard about the potluck dinner? I've been wanting to discuss it with you."

"Heard about it. Wouldn't have wanted to be there, thanks very much. I heard things were said about locker room cruelty, and how the younger generation suffered, also, because of what I wrote."

"They did suffer, Dad. You should have taken more care to disguise the details."

"I thought I had. Those were composite, fictionalized cases. I didn't lift my brother and his kids wholesale and put them in my books. To the extent that I did use them, I've apologized for it over and over again. Or I've tried to. And I'm tired of it now."

"They saw themselves in those cases."

"They were wrong. I had an argument to make. I had hundreds of cases to draw on. I drew details from so many different sources, *no one* could truthfully say that I'd plucked them out of life and put them on a page. People always think that way about writers, whether its fiction or psychology. *You put me in your book,* they say. I did not do anything of the kind. People don't have the slightest clue how the process works."

Suddenly, he sounded like an old man, and Jake felt a pang of concern. He looked pale, his hair had more salt than pepper in it now, and he was leaning on his cluttered desk as if exhausted or in pain. Did Dad have health problems he wasn't talking about?

Maybe I should confront Abigail and demand some answers, Jake thought, because this doesn't seem right.

"Dad, are you okay?" He put his hand on his father's shoulder.

"I'm fine."

"Sit!"

"I will if you will." He returned, moving slowly, to the high-backed swivel chair at his desk, while Jake took a pile of file folders from the seat of a leather armchair and sat there. "Regrets tire a person out," his father continued after a moment, still speaking fretfully. "They're so unfinished."

"So you do have regrets about the books?"

"Of course I do! If my brother would only talk to me about it, we could heal this, but I can't see that it's ever going to happen, despite what Jillian is trying to do, and it's unfinished, and it's like my damned arthritis. It aches worse when the weather's bad. I thought we might have another chance three years ago, after they found Robbie, but— How is Robbie?" He suddenly asked.

"He's good. He's great. From what I've seen. We've run into each other at the hospital a couple of times. His wife is a really nice woman."

Jake remembered Nancy expressing a vague feeling of concern at the potluck dinner. She'd watched her husband a little too closely, not with a newlywed's pleasure but with an aura of anxiety and foreboding. He hadn't felt he knew her well enough to ask her about it, and he didn't want to add to his father's dark mood by mentioning it now, but he wondered what it was that she feared.

He said instead, quite abruptly, "Dad, what kind of regrets do you think haunt people the most, in your experience? Regret for the things they didn't do, or for the things they did?"

His father laughed. His color looked better now, thank goodness. "If you mean, 'I'm sorry I didn't kill my wife,' versus, 'I'm sorry I did,' people tend to voice the second statement far more often. But if you're talking more about 'I'm sorry I didn't go to college'..."

"Yeah, things like that."

"Most people regret their own lack of courage more than they ever regret an act of bravery that didn't pan out." He looked sharply at Jake, and Jake decided the man wasn't anywhere near getting old and frail, he was sharp as a damned tack. "We're talking about you, here, aren't we?"

"Hell, I'm that transparent?"

"Not often."

"So why now?"

"Because it's obviously important, whatever it is."

"I need to spill it, in that case, don't I?"

"Since I think it's why you came..." Dad suggested gently.

Okay, Dad.

Right again.

Fifteen minutes later, Jake finished his tale. "…and I think it's gotten worse over the years, not better. I mean, the grief has eased. She was so little, Dad, it's hard to imagine the…the *woman* she'd be by now. Anna, our tiny little baby, as a grown woman." He shook his head. "See? I can't picture it. But the fear of the grief…of ever going through it again, of letting Stacey down, of being locked together, the two of us, by misery and loss instead of joined by happiness…"

"So you'll be happy and free of grief and loss and fear if you walk away?"

"Hell, no!"

"So you're stuck, aren't you? Potentially miserable with Stacey, or potentially miserable without her. I know which option I'd go for."

"I can't."

"You keep saying that. It's a self-fulfilling prophecy, if ever I heard one. You love her, don't you?"

"It's like an incurable disease."

"Stop thinking like a damned doctor, and start thinking like a human being. You only get one life, Jake. Live it. Sprint headlong toward it without a safety helmet, dive over the edge and experience the rush."

"I've told you. John did that. He rushed in,

pushed both of them into something that was wrong, made promises he couldn't keep. She deserves better."

"You're not like John."

"You've met the man?"

"You're not like anyone, Jake. You're you. And Stacey loves you. It's lasted more than seventeen years with little encouragement. You have to go back to that hospital, Jake, and you know it. You have to walk in to the Pediatric Unit with the right expression on your face and the right feeling in your heart even if every muscle in your body is screaming for you to run away, even if you think you're going to yell at the staff or throw up or cry or all three things at once, and you have to tell Stacey that you love her and you're there. Permanently."

"I—"

I can't.

He pressed his hands over his face and his closed eyes, still lost.

"Because from what you've said," his father went on ruthlessly, "if you don't do it today, you might not get another chance. Do you think no one else is scared about these things? You somehow think that the fear you gave in to seventeen years ago—when you were not much more than a boy—is unique to you, a fatal flaw in your character that disqualifies you from ever trying again."

Jake took his hands away and lifted his head. His whole body tingled and every hair stood on end. The words struck a chord.

Yes, of course he thought that! Wouldn't anybody?

His father looked at him. "It doesn't! There's a quote…" He swiveled around at his desk and began scrabbling through a pile of files.

"Don't give me a quote, Dad," Jake groaned. His throat felt tight as a vise and his eyes stung.

"I have it right here, somewhere."

"Could you maybe remember it?" His voice came out scratchy, cynical and tired. "From your head? Even if it's not word for word?"

"Here it is. I knew I had it." He read proudly, "'The brave man is not he who feels no fear, For that were stupid and irrational; But he, whose noble soul its fear subdues, And bravely dares the danger nature shrinks from.' Joanna Baillie, Scottish poet, from the play—"

"Thank you, Dad."

"You can have the printout."

"Thanks, again."

"Son…" He stood, pulled Jake to his feet with a strength he shouldn't still have, and hugged him. "Stop thinking. Just do what your heart wants, and you'll find you're ready for it. Have faith."

"Stacey said that." His voice was muffled by the shoulder of his father's sweater.

"Stacey's right." He let Jake go. "Is that lasagne I can smell?"

"Just the remnants, possibly. For a skinny girl, Suzie seemed pretty hungry when I got here."

"You staying to eat?"

"No. I'm not."

"Going back to the hospital?"

Jake sighed. "I—I don't know."

Chapter Fourteen

"Go, John, seriously, it's fine."

"I wouldn't, if—"

"I know you wouldn't head back to Olympia if there was any real concern. And I know your meeting tomorrow is important." Stacey repeated what they both had been told. "The strep throat swab came back negative, and they don't think this is meningitis, either, because his condition has stabilized now instead of getting worse. We just have to wait for a doctor to see them and sign their discharge paperwork, but the staff are pretty busy, and the twins are comfortable."

"I think Ella's drifting off, now," John said. Max was already sleeping.

"It may take a while, but there's no need for you to wait."

"Okay, then. Thanks. I'll call you when I get in, okay?" He gave her a swift kiss on the temple and left, and she let out a gust of breath as he disappeared.

She cared about him—and always would—but she felt so much more like herself when he wasn't around, so much more grounded. They drained each other's energy, and could manage to give so little in return. The twins had been their best gift to each other in the end.

She checked them.

Yes, Ella was asleep, finally—the medication had brought her fever down, and Max's, too.

Stacey realized vaguely that she was hungry. It must be after eight o'clock in the evening, but she didn't want to leave the twins so her stomach would have to wait. For hours, probably. Even if the discharge formalities happened quickly, she still had to drive home, get the twins settled for the night. Not that they'd sleep through when they were sick. She would be up every couple of hours, probably.

Her tired mind suddenly circled back to the subject of driving home, and she realized she didn't have a car. She'd driven here with John, and now he'd gone, taking his set of car seats with him. She'd have to take a cab and check when she ordered it that it had toddler seats available.

Which would be easy enough and shouldn't feel like the last straw on the camel's back of this difficult weekend, but somehow it did.

Jake should be here.

No matter what he'd said about impossible faith and promises, no matter how hopeless their future seemed, he should be here.

The ache of emotional hunger and emptiness inside her was far worse than the ache in her empty stomach. She wanted his body to lean against, his voice reassuring her or distracting her with humor, his SUV with Max and Ella's car seats still strapped in the back from Friday night because both of them had totally forgotten to get them out.

She just wanted him, the way she always had.

But he'd felt out of place…or he just hadn't wanted to be here…and so he'd gone, and she didn't know if he planned to come back.

She closed her eyes, knowing she'd just have to live through the next few hours heartbeat by heartbeat, ignoring any needs of her own, focused only on her children. She could do it. She'd done it before. The rewards came at other times, in other ways, and were worth all of this.

Several minutes went by.

Her neck ached and her back stiffened on the uncomfortable plastic hospital chair. Max whimpered in his sleep, then settled again. She wished she could turn the lights down lower, but Max and Ella had been kept here in the open pediatric room where the patients in four other beds needed the bright light when staff came to work over them.

She closed her eyes again.

Then she heard a voice. "Stace?"

Jake had come back. Her eyes flashed open because she couldn't quite believe it—she needed visual confirmation. The collar of his jacket was turned up and his ears and nose looked cold. His eyes seemed darker than usual and his mouth was set in a tight line, but he was so *right*, standing there looking down at her, she didn't have room in her head or her heart to think too clearly about what it meant. His presence simply made her happy.

And somewhere nearby, something smelled good.

"Hi…" she said creakily.

"Where's John?"

"He left. The throat swabs came back negative, and Max's fever responded well to medication. They don't think it's meningitis, just a common virus or the start of a bad cold. We're going home when someone gets round to discharging us."

"That's fantastic! Oh, lord, Stacey, that's so good!" He bent down and hugged her, and she had to suck back a sob. She wanted so badly to kiss him. No. For him to kiss her. Just sweep her up into his arms and kiss her breathless with relief and happiness and promise "But... John left?" he said instead.

"I told him it was okay. He has a big meeting tomorrow."

He looked as if he wanted to say something more, but then changed tack. "I brought you some of my stepmother's lasagne. I thought you might be hungry."

"That's what I can smell?"

"She's a good cook. I had to fight my stepsister for the last piece. It's hot, and there's a fork and a napkin and a bottle of juice. I considered a hip flask full of bourbon, too, but decided that could be overkill. Oh, and I have the kids' seats still in my car. In a minute I'll find the doctor and get this discharge taken care of and we can go home."

She burst into shaky tears. "Oh, Jake..."

He took her properly into his arms this time, laughing. "You hate lasagne that much?"

"I love lasagne."

"Good."

"And I love you for thinking to bring it." She hugged him.

"You thought I'd let you go hungry? I knew you wouldn't leave them to go eat."

"I just…love you, Jake. I don't know why you came back, but—but…" She couldn't go on.

"Shh, why do you think I came back?"

"To bring me dinner?" She looked up into his face, knowing what he was going to say but needing to hear it as many times as he wanted to say it.

"Because I love you," he whispered. Then he gave a crooked smile. "I know, I know. I've always loved you and it's never been enough…."

"Why, Jake?"

"Because I was so scared I'd let you down. I'm still scared but apparently that's normal."

She laughed. *"Apparently?"*

"Dad read me this quote about bravery and fear. *Gave* me this quote. Forced me at gunpoint to fold up the printout of the quote and put it in my wallet, and I think he might have personally tattooed it to my chest if he'd had the right equipment."

"You had a narrow escape. I had no idea quotes could be so powerful."

"Neither did I. But the talk we had was pretty good. I'm still scared, Stace. Anna's still there in my heart, reminding me of all the ways this could be hard—the ways it *will* be hard, at some point, inevitably, over the next fifty years—"

"Fifty years?" she whispered.

"—but I can't let you go. My Dad's right. You're right. You deserve everything I can promise, and I have to make the promises on pure faith. And I want to make them if you want to hear them."

"Oh, I do!"

"Marry me, Stacey. I want us to take care of each other for the rest of our lives and make this right, at last. The twins need a full-time father as well as a part-time one, and every time I see them I care about them more. By the time we have a baby of our own, there'll be no difference in my heart."

"A baby of our own?" she whispered.

"We need a baby of our own. I want to see you blossoming with pregnancy, I want to be there with you and be happy with you at the birth. And if we can't be biological parents together, we can adopt and that baby will be our own just as much. All our kids I'll love with everything I have. I realized you were right about the precious little daughter we lost. I don't want Anna to be the reason I could never love another child. That hurts her memory. Even though you said it to me, I never saw it until tonight, never felt it in my heart, but suddenly it was so clear. I drove away from Dad's place and stopped somewhere and just sat in the car, thinking about everything and it fell into place. I guess you've known all of this for a long time."

"Yes, oh, yes, I have and I didn't know how to help you see it. I wanted to say it to you in better, clearer words, but I didn't know how."

"I don't think you could have said it any better. Not in a way I could have understood before I was ready to. I don't know why none of it fell into place until now." He brushed her mouth in a soft kiss. "Actually, yes, I do. Because I needed you back in my life first."

"Don't make me take all the credit," she whispered. "Share it."

"Only because I want to share everything with you from now on."

Sharing her life with Jake. It sounded so good. Stacey started smiling and couldn't stop until Jake kissed her slow and deep and sweet. Beside them, the twins slept, unaware of how much their little lives had just changed. The delicious aroma of the lasagne wafted once again into Stacey's awareness.

This was what families were all about, she knew. What life was all about. The scariness of hospitals tempered by the taste of comfort food. The power of love, so much stronger than the power of fear or hate. Faith and responsibilities and promises and rewards. Rifts that could heal, feelings that could change and grow.

"Marry me, Stacey," Jake whispered.

"Yes! Oh, yes!"

At last, seventeen years later than predicted, the Couple Most Likely To Marry Right Out Of High School had managed to get it right.

* * * * *

When Lisa Sanders falls for a wealthy real estate mogul, her secret past threatens to destroy her future. Can a new romance heal her old wounds?
Don't miss
FALLING FOR THE TEXAS TYCOON
by Karen Rose Smith
The next installment of the new
Special Edition Continuity
LOGAN'S LEGACY REVISITED
On sale February 2007
wherever Silhouette Books are sold

Happily ever after is just the beginning...

Turn the page for a sneak preview of
DANCING ON SUNDAY AFTERNOONS
by
Linda Cardillo

Harlequin Everlasting—Every great love
has a story to tell.™
A brand-new line from Harlequin Books
launching this February!

Prologue

Giulia D'Orazio
1983

I had two husbands—Paolo and Salvatore.

Salvatore and I were married for thirty-two years. I still live in the house he bought for us; I still sleep in our bed. All around me are the signs of our life together. My bedroom window looks out over the garden he planted. In the middle of the city, he coaxed tomatoes, peppers, zucchini—even grapes for his wine— out of the ground. On weekends, he used to drive up to his cousin's farm in Waterbury and bring back manure. In the winter, he wrapped the peach tree and the fig tree with rags and black rubber hoses against the cold, his massive, coarse hands gentling those trees as if they were his fragile-skinned babies. My neighbor, Dominic Grazza, does that for me now. My boys have no time for the garden.

In the front of the house, Salvatore planted roses. The roses I take care of myself. They are giant, cream-colored, fragrant. In the afternoons, I like to sit out on the porch with my coffee, protected from the eyes of the neighborhood by that curtain of flowers.

Salvatore died in this house thirty-five years ago. In the last months, he lay on the sofa in the parlor so he could be in the middle of everything. Except for the two oldest boys, all the children were still at home and we ate together every evening. Salvatore could see the dining room table from the sofa, and he could hear everything that was said. "I'm not dead, yet," he told me. "I want to know what's going on."

When my first grandchild, Cara, was born, we brought her to him, and he held her on his chest, stroking her tiny head. Sometimes they fell asleep together.

Over on the radiator cover in the corner of the

parlor is the portrait Salvatore and I had taken on our twenty-fifth anniversary. This brooch I'm wearing today, with the diamonds—I'm wearing it in the photograph also—Salvatore gave it to me that day. Upstairs on my dresser is a jewelry box filled with necklaces and bracelets and earrings. All from Salvatore.

I am surrounded by the things Salvatore gave me, or did for me. But, God forgive me, as I lie alone now in my bed, it is Paolo I remember.

Paolo left me nothing. Nothing, that is, that my family, especially my sisters, thought had any value. No house. No diamonds. Not even a photograph.

But after he was gone, and I could catch my breath from the pain, I knew that I still had something. In the middle of the night, I sat alone and held them in my hands, reading the words over and over until I heard his voice in my head. I had Paolo's letters.

* * * * *

Be sure to look for
DANCING ON SUNDAY AFTERNOONS
available January 30, 2007.
And look, too, for our other
Everlasting title available,
FALL FROM GRACE by Kristi Gold.

FALL FROM GRACE
is a deeply emotional story
of what a long-term love really means.
As Jack and Anne Morgan discover,
marriage vows can be broken—
but they can be mended, too.
And the memories of their marriage have
an unexpected power
to bring back a love that never really left....

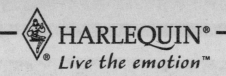

HARLEQUIN®
INTRIGUE®

BREATHTAKING ROMANTIC SUSPENSE

Shared dangers and passions lead to electrifying romance and heart-stopping suspense!

Every month, you'll meet six new heroes who are guaranteed to make your spine tingle and your pulse pound. With them you'll enter into the exciting world of Harlequin Intrigue— where your life is on the line and so is your heart!

THAT'S INTRIGUE— ROMANTIC SUSPENSE AT ITS BEST!

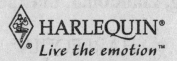

HARLEQUIN®
Live the emotion™

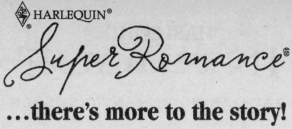
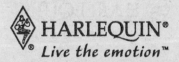

HARLEQUIN®
Presents

The world's bestselling romance series...
The series that brings you your favorite authors,
month after month:

Helen Bianchin...Emma Darcy
Lynne Graham...Penny Jordan
Miranda Lee...Sandra Marton
Anne Mather...Carole Mortimer
Susan Napier...Michelle Reid

and many more uniquely talented authors!

Wealthy, powerful, gorgeous men...
Women who have feelings just like your own...
The stories you love, set in exotic, glamorous locations...

HARLEQUIN®
Presents

Seduction and Passion Guaranteed!